BELINDA CRAWFORD

DEMONS & Battleskirts

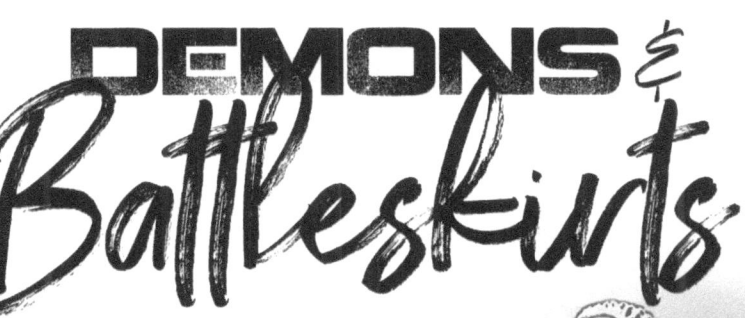

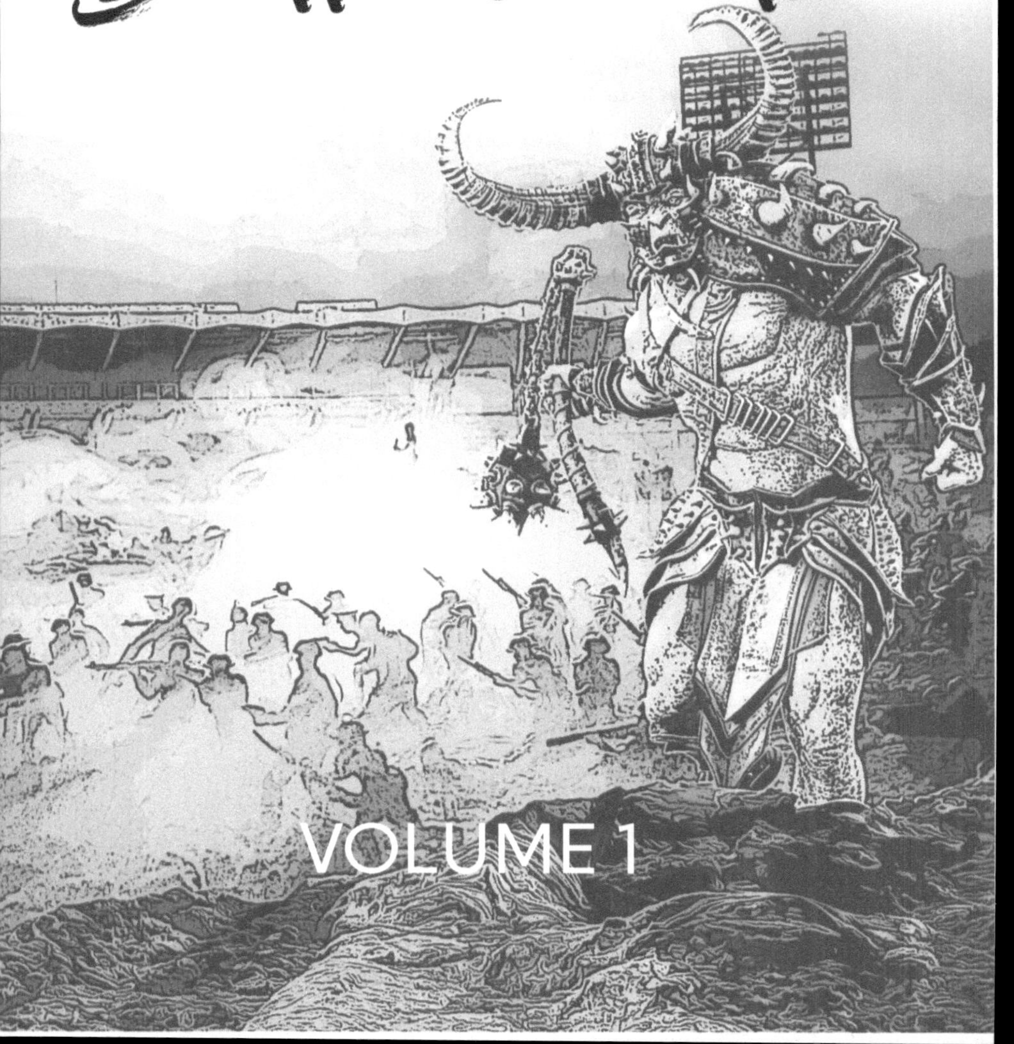

VOLUME 1

HENDRIX & FAUST
PUBLISHERS

Published by Hendrix & Faust, Publishers in 2023

www.belindacrawford.com

ISBN: 978-0-6450459-7-0 (ebook)
ISBN: 978-0-6450459-8-7 (paperback)

To Iffet B,
a gem among Heroes.

Byrne

Chapter 1

The spike rammed through the demon's chest-plate with a wet *crack*, its black ichor splattering across her boots, some reaching high enough to eat into the nano-mail covering her legs. Still more of it ate at the rich, black silk of her thigh-length battleskirt and the longer drop of her tabard. It seemed to devour the warriors' creed embroidered in silver thread down the tabard's length, with particular relish.

More of the acidic, black blood sizzled against the thin sheen of her personal shield, the magic weaker now than at the start of the battle, retreating from her arms and legs to concentrate around her torso and head. It would breach the shield soon, but the intricately carved plates of armour covering her chest and shoulders would keep the demon blood at bay. At least until the sun rose, after that... the bright yellow rays of dawn would finish the fight.

At her feet, the demon wrapped two of its three sets of hands around her weapon's haft, mandibles splayed wide over the sharp points of its lipless mouth. It stared at her with defiance in its venomous green eyes. The muscles under its thick, yellow-black armour bulged as it tried to push the glaive out of its chest, even as it raked her armour-clad legs with its other two hands, the thick tips of its claws adding a horrid screech to the cacophony of the battlefield.

She snarled back, teeth bared, matching its green stare with the obsidian fury of hers, and tightened her grip on the weapon. Under her hands, Ahriman *pulsed*, the once-golden metal long since tarnished by the shadows rising from her soul, the runes carved into the metal writhing with the dark. Just like the blade on the other end, a dark crescent blazing over the battlefield.

Az pushed the glaive's spiked end deeper into the demon's chest and twisted. She relished the thick, soggy *crunch* as the glaive broke through the creature's softer, inner shell before it ripped through its innards and punctured its spine.

The demon gurgled once – all six of its hands still uselessly trying to prevent the inevitable – and died.

A yank. Bits of carapace flew through the air, more blood staining her legs, trying to sink through the nano-mail behind her knees, the smooth shine of armour-reinforced boots. Az was already spinning, Ahriman twisting in her hands, an extension not just of her arms and feet but her will, her soul, the essence of her being, the blazing crescent blade as hungry for blood as she.

A head flew. A horn. Hand. An arm. Ichor sprayed in black arcs across the predawn, outlined starker and deeper under the glaring lights of the football field. The carefully tended green lawn turned to mud, shredded by talons and scorched by fireballs. The three-metre-high goals at either end had been little more than toothpicks before the eel-headed Valous demons, the posts shattering as the bus-sized flyers were brought down one-by-one by her sister's magic.

A Mammoth demon lay face down in the mud, its trunk-like

limbs flung to the winds. One chest-sized hand was still wrapped around a huge energy blaster, the demon's back a smoking ruin of bone and gore, blown to bits when the generator strapped there exploded. And of the seats...

The once pristine bleachers were broken and bloody, demon blood eating through plastic as readily as metal, monstrous corpses strewn over the white seats like forgotten sweaters.

A final slash, a blood-curdling scream fit to shred her ears.

Az spun, Ahriman a whirl of pain and metal in her hands, the shadows embedded in its haft still ravenous for more. But there were no more demons. The ruined football field was desolate, littered with corpses and the final pained moans of the not-yet-dead. Only the last fleeting shapes of the Horde remained; stragglers melting into darkness, fleeing under the bleachers and the scraggy dusk of the old industrial park beyond, desperate to outrun the coming dawn.

She roared, thwarted anger and bloodlust pouring from her throat, the shadows in her soul spilling out her mouth in a promise of retribution. There would be no escape, no place the horned and taloned host could hide.

Tellamoth wouldn't escape her again.

Az gathered herself, the cold power rising through her bones, dark magic coalescing in her hands—

The soft shimmer of bells was all the warning she had.

As quickly as it came, the dark, cold magic retreated within, raising goosebumps over her skin. Az turned as moonbeams coalesced, shoving Ahriman between her and the light as if its thin shadow could protect her from the pale rays barely visible beneath the flickering floodlights.

Della stepped out of moonlight. Tall and proud, her dark mahogany hair a corkscrew cloud about her head. She shone with power. From the delicate tattoos bisecting her eyes and flowing over her cheeks, to the gem-like stone held in the tarnished silver swirl atop her staff, she glowed with the intense azure of rampant magic. The power of the High Priestess shimmered from her pores.

For a moment, before the moonbeams faded, the darkness in Az's soul screeched. Pain wracked her being, a thousand tiny slivers digging into the fabric of her self, piercing the shadows until all that was left... all that was left was—

'Byrne.' Della grabbed Az's arm, but it was the name of the girl lurking deep in the shadows of Az's mind, that stabbed. 'The battle's over, you have to come.'

The bright-blue magic faded, light retreating from Della's face and neck like water flowing downhill, disappearing under her fitted chest-plate to the back of her hand, flooding into her staff. The High Priestess's armour was more filigree than plate, as unlikely to stop a pulse ray as her long, ground-length tabard and spilt skirts were to not get underfoot.

Az ripped herself away, spinning from the High Priestess. Even with Ahriman between them, Della's magic still burned. Magic may no longer have coursed through the azure lines inked onto every inch of Della's body, but it lingered. A painful glow that assaulted Az's eyes, reaching through the thin, black membrane to haul the little girl – Byrne, her other self – from the darkness within.

She wouldn't let the girl rise. *Couldn't* let the girl rise. She had to find Tellamoth, had to end this *now*.

The High Priestess grabbed her arm again. Long, golden-brown fingers – each one banded with two tarnished silver rings – wrapped around her bicep. Magic still played around Della's hand, eating through Az's skin to the shadows swirling in her soul.

Az pulled the shadows tighter within, sensed the girl – Byrne – scream as the cold-dark left claw marks in her psyche, but she couldn't let the Priestess see. Not yet. Not when she had just awakened; before she had the strength to confront the blaze of the Priestess's power.

'Sword,' the High Priestess said, using her other name this time, the title that called not to the girl but the fury and bloodlust of the self she was now. Or the small part of herself, the tiny sliver she had pushed through the barrier the girl kept between them.

The strength of the barrier had surprised her, the determination of such a young, ignorant soul. Of course, the soul was still hers, still Az's, one of the scattered fragments left after the Wheel ripped the Az of before into tiny little pieces – the shining example of heroism and righteousness flung across the Universe.

'Enough,' the Priestess continued. Her voice echoed with power, resounding through the air with the force of a mighty gong. 'The Horde is broken and Nova needs you, you have to come.'

'No.' The denial broke from Az's lips, and the sound of her own voice almost shocked her back into the dark, almost allowed the girl to rise. It was deep and guttural and hoarse, tasted like blood on the back of her tongue, ached like the first microns of acidic blood eating through the nano-mail at her knee.

It shocked Della too. Else why would the High Priestess loosen her grip, the power under her skin dulling for just a second.

A second was all it took, all that was needed for Az to launch herself into the fading dredges of night, Ahriman held tight at her side, the industrial park's high wire fence and cracked concrete—

Azure light blazed and Az screamed.

Agony engulfed her, took the air from her lungs, the iron from her knees. Inside, the darkness turned to acid, was a hundred glass-taloned Caroen demons ripping into her soul, and outside... Outside the light forced her down, down, down, past her knees until her face was in the wet dirt, until the musty smell of it was in her nose and still it pushed, sank her deeper. Into the darkness itself, into the bone-chilling cold where there was no sight, no sound, nothing at all. Except the girl.

The girl. The tiny fragment of herself with its desperate, naive desire to *live*, rose as Az descended. For a heartbeat, as the acid and claws hacked at the threads of her sanity, the Priestess's brilliant blue light weighing her down, they passed each other. So alike, the same rounded face, the large brown-black eyes, the long nose and pale, yellow-gold skin. The same determination too, turning the soft bow-shaped lips hard and dimpling the point of her chin.

The girl—

Byrne pushed past Az, imagining her boots in the other's face as she caught the azure light in her hands and thrust upwards. A sharp *snap*. A jerk in her middle, and she was Byrne again, her other self – Az – trapped under the thin membrane that divided them.

It was Byrne who pushed herself off the torn ground, who lifted herself out of the mud. The wet, ichor-stained earth plastered to her chest even as it stuck to her cheek. It was Byrne who wrapped both hands around Ahriman's haft, her touch that banished the shadows clinging to its runes, and levered herself to her feet, shaking and cold but free.

'Byrne?' With a long, elegant finger under her chin, Della lifted Byrne's gaze. Power once again blazed in the lines over Della's cheeks and from the gem-like circle in the middle of her forehead, and there was lightning in her big dark eyes.

Byrne spared one hand from Ahriman to clasp Della's.

'Byrne,' her best friend said again, the dark wings of her brows rising with hope. 'Is that you?'

Byrne nodded. 'Yes,' she said, her voice strange to her ears with its hoarse croak. She cleared her throat, the muscles sore and the flesh raw from Az's harsh battlecries. The copper tang of blood mixed with the mud on her tongue as she straightened her shoulders, swallowed, and tried again. 'It's me. Take me to Nova.'

Pain crossed Della's face, weighing at the corners of her full red lips, while sorrow dulled the crack of lightning in her eyes. 'It's bad,' she said, even as she clasped Byrne's hand tighter and moonbeams gathered around them.

'I know,' was all Byrne said as the world disappeared.

Chapter

It was worse than bad. It was its own blood-soaked hell.

Double lockers lined either side of the girls' narrow locker room. The small metal boxes had once been stacked in neat rows, one atop the other, and while the paint on their navy-blue fronts had been chipped and scratched from decades of hard use, and the dark wooden benches down the centre were old and worn, they'd been neat. Sturdy. Efficient.

Now, the locker were doors crumpled and scored, entire sections pulled from the walls – bits of concrete still attached to the heavy, metal bolts that had secured them to the off-white concrete. Of the banks that remained upright, most bore scorch marks, the heat of whatever magic had been unleashed causing the navy paint to bubble. A few were torn, the metal ripped, edges melted like butter.

Benches were little more than kindling; the old, glossy wood crunched under Byrne's boots, splinters skidding from under her heels. Most had shattered under impact – a fist, a sword, a body – but some smouldered, the wooden planks scorched black either by lightning or fire, she couldn't tell which. It filled the air with the bitter taste of ash, mixing with the damp, musty scent of old sweat and water.

The floor had fared little better. The small grey tiles smashed, the grout between them – in so many varying shades of brown and black, no one had ever really been able to tell what colour it had started out as – pulverised. The blackboard beside the archway leading to the showers still stood though, the flyers covering its surface only slightly charred.

For all the violence done to metal and concrete, it was the blood that chilled Byrne's spine. The thick red trail started at the end of the room, just a few short strides from the arch that lead to the showers. It shouldn't have been as visible as it was, mixed in amongst the detritus, should have been just another wet shadow in the valley of destruction, and yet... And yet it screamed at her, riveted her gaze and made her feet leaden, made her heart beat hard and heavy in her chest.

Della was already there, standing in the arch, pain and sorrow still creasing her brow and tugging at her lips. The other girl didn't say anything, but the weight in her gaze, the way she waited – patient yet expecting – drew Byrne forward, one heavy step at a time.

Beyond the archway, it was... normal. No shattered tiles, no stench of ash or burned metal. Six shower cubicles stood straight and unmolested, thin plastic curtains pulled neatly to the side, the beige privacy screens separating them unmarked by violence. Only the blood gave lie to normalcy; that, and Fion waiting like a silent mourner at the other end of the aisle.

Fion, the Executioner, stood at the end farthest from the door, arms crossed over her chest, the long blonde tail of her intricately braided mohawk blackened by the same blood crusting Byrne's legs. The other girl looked up in a slow, jerky motion, like the effort to tear her gaze from whatever lay in the last cubicle hurt. Perhaps it did. Tears had made tracks down her face, long black lines of mascara running through the grime, and she had her thumb between her teeth, ripping into the nail until it bled.

Walking down that aisle was like walking towards a grave.

But was it Nova's funeral she attended, or her own?

The thought skittered through Byrne's mind as the hard soles of her boots echoed in the small, musty-smelling space, and deep in her being, under the thin membrane that kept her other self down, Az snarled defiance.

Not this time, Az said.

Byrne ignored her.

Fion stepped back, pressing into the tiled wall, almost sucking in her gut to let Byrne pass. There was fear in the movement, a tiny thrilling spike that sped Byrne's pulse even as it sank into her heart.

As she passed, Byrne was aware of Fion reaching out, of Della wrapping the other girl in her arms, but most of her attention was on the bloody tangle of limbs slumped under the shower.

Suun knelt beside their sister, her long midnight hair a river down her back, barely a strand out of place despite the soot that marked the pale beige of her cheeks and the blood that stained the intricate, lacy armour across her shoulders. The leaves of her knee-length skirts parted around her on the tiles, soaking up their sister's blood. She held glowing hands over Nova's chest, expression tight with strain as she fought to keep Nova alive. How much longer Suun could, Byrne didn't know. Their sister was... mangled.

Nova's legs were stretched out before her. One boot was gone, exposing the talon marks ripping her leg from calf to thigh, bone gleaming a stark white amidst bloody flesh, while her other leg... Byrne swallowed.

The lower half bent the wrong way, as if someone had taken a sledgehammer to her sister's shin, snapping it in the middle.

The damage continued the farther up Byrne dragged her gaze. Nova's golden battleskirt and the skin-tight nano-mail armour underneath were shredded, the bloody marks in her sister's skin too neat to have been made by claws. One shoulder hung awkwardly and there were bones where her hand should have been, her forearm ending in a cauterised stump.

'How long?' Byrne's words came out confident, smooth, betraying none of the turmoil building in her chest. The fear, the horror. The anger.

So much anger rising not just in the hot wave from her own gut but seeping through the membrane that separated her from the other. So much anger, and not all of it aimed at the man who'd butchered her sister, because she knew what came next, what had to come next, even as every bit of her railed against it.

Inside, Az snarled, raking talons against the barrier, her fury cold and dark as the shadows in which she roiled. *I won't do it again*, she said.

What, Byrne didn't ask, because deep down, in the place beyond Az, amongst the nightmares that lived in the cold-dark that forced her screaming from sleep, she knew. And she agreed.

She agreed, and that thought, more than her sister's broken and bloodied body, was terrifying.

She wouldn't do it again.

Suun didn't look up. 'I can keep her alive long enough for the paramedics to get here. Maybe to get her to Emergency.' She tore her focus from her work and pinned Byrne with large, dark-hickory eyes. Fear lurked in the downturned depths and pinched the smooth skin between ebony brows, before Suun wiped the emotion from her face. She turned her attention back to Nova. 'Not much longer than that.'

'Long enough,' Nova said. Her sister's head lolled, but she straightened it, gazing at Byrne with eyes that had once blazed like the sun but were now a dull brown. Blood bubbled at her mouth, the froth trickling down her chin to drip onto her chest and pool around the shattered remnants of the golden medallion that should have protected her.

There was only one way to break a medallion, only one way to get through the magic protecting it, and the knowledge burned.

'I told you. I told you not to trust him.' The words left Byrne's mouth, ripe with the resentment and pain writhing in her chest, acidic as demon blood. 'When will you listen?'

Nova smiled, revealing the gaping holes where her front teeth should have been. 'In another lifetime, sister.'

Resentment flared to anger and Byrne darted forward, boots splashing in the mix of water and her sister's blood as she crouched at Nova's side. 'This *is* another lifetime.'

'Then I will listen in the next.'

In the next. The words shivered in Byrne's bones, made the darkness writhe and twist.

Deep inside, Az snarled.

'No,' she said, and wasn't sure if it was just her or Az rising through the membrane that kept them apart. Byrne shook her head. 'No, not again. I won't let you.'

'You can't stop me, sister.' Nova coughed, her blood splattering over Byrne's face. She drew a ragged breath. 'It's my right, and you swore an oath.'

Nova looked past her, and Byrne knew, without turning, that Della was there, arms raised, her staff coalescing out of nothing, the azure tattoos on her face and arms blazing with the power gathering around her.

The force of it stirred the dark fall of hair down Byrne's back, lifted the charred strands around her face. Even Suun's hair lifted and flapped, the bloodstained ends of Nova's waist-length locks joining them – the three of them so much alike and yet so different. Soon, Della's spell would join them all into one, would whip hair and skirts into a tornado, and the maelstrom of the High Priestess's power would be unstoppable.

Byrne gripped Nova's uninjured shoulder. 'I don't want this. Stop the ritual. Please.'

Nova looked at her. There was pain in her gold eyes, weariness and sympathy mixed with a bone-deep sorrow that sunk hooks into Byrne's heart, but determination hardened her gaze. 'I know,' she said. 'And no.'

No. No, no, no.

The denial echoed. Its grim, steely resolve reverberated inside Byrne's skull, her chest. Her soul.

No.

Inside, the darkness surged, and she didn't stop it, didn't press back and down on the thin membrane between her and it, between her and *Az*. The dark rose, a tidal wave with Az at its crest, bursting through the barrier, wrapping around her heart, flowing through her bones, taking over her eyes.

Blood and water froze around her boots.

There was no blood left in Nova's face, but her eyes widened until white ringed the faded gold. 'Byrne?'

'I won't go back there,' she said, or maybe Az said it, their voices melding, impossible to tell one from the other. She wasn't sure if she was talking to herself or to Nova, didn't know if the light bathing her face was the magic in Suun's hands or something else, the power in her own core, the destruction she worked so hard to keep contained. The violence, the rage. It didn't matter. All that mattered was the wind at her back, was the knife she could *feel* in Fion's grip. Was the blood spurting from Nova's severed hand. Was the darkness.

Was the bone-destroying cold.

'Not again.' The words lifted Byrne to her feet. 'Not ever.'

Ahriman was there, forming out of nothingness, the comforting weight of it, the gleam of the crescent blade. She was spinning, knocking back Fion's rush, the golden knife spinning from the other girl's hand. And then there was her best friend, shining with power, the brilliant marks of the High Priestess burning under her skin, azure against brown.

The darkness screeched, the azure eating at Byrne's insides, but the pain was nothing, *nothing* to what waited beyond the ritual.

Nova was screaming, her desperation trying to pull at Byrne's muscles, to hold Ahriman back, but the weapon had its own weight.

Surprise widened Della's eyes.

Ahriman found Della's gut.

Chapter 3

Four months ago.

'Nova's at it again,' Della said as she squeezed into the old leather Chesterfield like it was a lounge made for three instead of a slightly oversized armchair tucked into a corner of the Kadar Academy's mammoth library.

Byrne scooted over without protest. If she'd wanted to hide, there were better places deep in the endless rows of old wooden bookshelves. In cosy chairs just like this one tucked away in little alcoves all over the place, each with conveniently placed reading lights and little tables to sit a water bottle or coffee. She could have found peace from the whispers that trailed in her wake, but peace was a luxury Byrne no longer had.

Instead, she smoothed the navy pleats of her school skirt back under as Della squished in, throwing legs in knee-high white socks over Byrne's black stockinged ones.

Della's white collared blouse pulled a little tighter over her chest with the move, exposing the pendant at her throat; the rich blue stone wrapped in its delicate filigree of golden wires shaped to look like a tree, a vibrant contrast to the dark bronze of her skin.

The pendant hidden under Byrne's school blouse warmed at

Della

the other's nearness, and her hand went to her chest, fingers seeking the upside-down crescent of their own accord.

This chair, right on the edge of the communal study area with its old wooden tables and ladder-back chairs, let her peer over the top of her history book to where Nova held court.

'They're like moths to the sun,' Della said, her gaze, like Byrne's, on the long study table near the big windows overlooking the quadrangle.

Books lay open on the honey-brown surface, but all eyes were on Nova. Even in Kadar's conservative uniform, with her midnight hair braided and her collar buttoned to her chin, Nova radiated a power that attracted others more surely than gravity.

She was not pretty, not in the way other girls were, not with her broad cheekbones, pale-gold skin and thick eyebrows over amber eyes. She was not rich – not by Kadar's standards where Bentleys were as common as Porches; and her family was neither powerful nor famous. But still, the boys and girls who could buy and sell Nova's entire life ten times over, gathered around her, pulled by the sheer force of her personality.

Byrne narrowed her gaze, trying for the thousandth time to pick it apart.

Perhaps it was Nova's confidence; Universe knew, she had never lacked for confidence. She had been an Empress after all, had commanded a thousand systems and every single one had knelt at her feet. Or been forced there.

Byrne's hand curled into a fist, remembering—

'There are already bets on which one she's going to pick,' Della said, interrupting Byrne's thought.

Two heads leaned closer to Nova than the others. Jacob Sully was the closest, long honey-blond hair flopping over his eyes, his finger trailing up Nova's shirtfront. Whatever he was saying drew a peal of laughter from her, one that engulfed the library in joy. Everyone except Nova's other suitor, Sebastian Becskei, whose arms crossed over his lean-muscled chest, couldn't quite keep his thick dark brows from scrunching over a broad nose.

Byrne snorted. 'She won't pick either of them.' And more fool anyone who thought otherwise.

Nova wasn't one to choose when she could have both, one for his brains, the other for his body. It would be up to Sully and Becskei to decide whether or not they were willing to share.

Della leaned in closer, a stray strand of mahogany hair tickling Byrne's cheek. 'I don't know, Jacob Sully is awful cute.'

He was also a mathlete, with a GPA of three-point-eight and a smart mouth to match. Perfect for Nova. It didn't matter that he wasn't the cutest boy in the school or that he didn't dash around the football field in tight pants or practice something as potentially lethal as fencing. That's what Becskei was for.

No, looks weren't the first thing Nova went for. Once, maybe, before the solar flare, but now... The people they were *before* were bleeding through, and for all her faults, the Empress had always known how to build alliances.

Seek out the strongest, the smartest and richest, and bind them to her with the most powerful motivation she could find. Once it had been fear, greed, and the kind of loyalty that was built over generations of rule. Now? Lust was a powerful thing.

That and the magic.

Almost imperceptible against the sunlight streaming through the window, power shimmered around Nova's fingers, sparkled in the air and haloed her in gold. The power of the Empress might have been invisible to those gathered around Nova, but that only made it more addictive and impossible to resist.

Frustration tightened Byrne's fist, or maybe it was anger. She couldn't tell anymore. The emotions wound around each other, impossible to pick apart, impossible to shed except for when she pounded a punching bag. Or a face.

'She used to be more subtle,' Della said, shifting in the seat. 'People are going to start noticing.'

Byrne wiggled over a bit more as Della snuggled into her side.

'I know,' she replied. The knowledge ate at her because she knew, deep down in the part of her that wasn't anger and bloodlust, that somewhere in this circus of teenage hormones and angst, Tellamoth lurked.

'Did you talk to her?'

'I tried.' She'd have had more luck talking sense into a dog.

'You should try again.'

'I'm not her nanny.'

'No, you're her older sister.'

The frown was automatic, scrunching Byrne's brow, tightening her jaw. 'Not in this lifetime, and even if I was, what difference would it make? The high and mighty Empress will do as she pleases.' And if her mightiness wasn't careful, she'd get them killed. But then that, too, was her right. Because she was the Empress and her word was more than law, it was Universal, part of the fabric of existence itself.

Woe be to anyone who disobeyed, who had a thought that contradicted Her mighty word. If not the Sword, then the Executioner would come for them, meeting out swift retribution at the end of a blade. Or fists.

Byrne's fists.

Fion's blade.

It was a little hard to hit herself in the face through, and Fion... Byrne sought out the other girl's blonde head.

Fion sat beside Suun at the long study table, hunched into herself, small and delicate, smiling softly as she basked in Nova's glow, same as the others. The all-powerful Executioner that had once been the scourge of a galaxy had tucked herself inside Fion's pale skin, hiding under baby pink sweaters and a voice too soft to scare a mouse.

If only the Sword was like that, if only she – Byrne – could push Az's pulsing darkness deep inside and hide her under torn jeans and anime t-shirts. If only it were that easy, that simple. Not that any of that would lessen Nova's power, her command. That was ingrained in Byrne's soul, in a place not even Az could reach. Or the darkness.

The darkness: another thing Nova had foisted on her, another force Nova would not acknowledge.

Paper crunched, shredded.

She looked down, tried to relax the fist shredding the history book.

'Hey.' Della nudged her side. 'Hey,' she said again, nudging Byrne's side. 'Look at me.'

Lips flat, trying and failing to hold back the resentment raging in her middle, Byrne turned to look her best friend in the eye.

Understanding shone there. 'It's okay,' she said. 'You're allowed to be upset. The dreams you've been having, they would upset anyone. You just have to be patient, she'll come around, she always does.'

No, she didn't. Not in time. Never in time. But Byrne didn't say that, just tucked the knowledge into that place where the Sword dwelled. 'Maybe,' she said instead.

'No maybes about it. She listens to you, even when you don't think she does.'

If only that were true, but the only person Nova listened to was Suun, her *real* sister in this lifetime, just as she had been in all the others. And Suun...

Byrne's gaze found the other girl, the youngest of them, and calm patience spilled out of those large hickory-coloured eyes the same way arrogance hugged Nova.

'I just...' Byrne rested her forehead against Della's. 'I'm scared, Della. The dreams are getting worse and this thing...' She pressed her fist against her chest, as if she could reach in and drag the ball of dread and darkness from it.

'They're just dreams, and this...?' Della poked her chest. 'That's indigestion. Seriously, girl, how much spaghetti did you scoff down at lunch? You know that stuff is going straight to your hips, right?'

'I work it off, unlike *some* of us.' She narrowed her eyes meaningfully at Della.

'Being gorgeous *is* a workout.'

'No, it's not.'

'The amount of time I spend on this hair, it's totally a workout.'

'Hey, your obsession with your locks is all on you; you don't *have* to get up at the crack of dawn to straighten it.'

'Says the girl with hair so straight she makes laser lines jealous.'

Byrne rolled her eyes. 'Whatever,' she said and stood.

Della grabbed her hand. 'Get down here, I'm not arguing with you while you're hovering.'

She plonked back down beside Della. 'I'm not hovering, I was leaving.'

'No, you're sitting here with me while we gossip about our fearless leader.' Della's eyes scooted over to the study table. 'I, for one, think she should ditch both of the current boy toys and set her eyes on *that* one.'

Byrne followed the direction of Della's azure fingernail.

A boy stood in the shadows of the farthest stacks. He was tall and slim, but something about the way his shirt tugged at his shoulders suggested the kind of lean musculature that came from work. Dark messy hair, pale-gold skin, a long sharp nose that he'd no doubt mastered the art of looking down.

He was facing the shelves, brows drawn over that hawk nose as he studied the spines. She'd seen him before, passed him in the halls, one of those faces glimpsed in the crowd but one she'd never talked to. He was good looking in a disapproving way, a challenge perhaps, even for Nova.

'Hmm,' Byrne murmured. 'He's a fifth year, isn't he?'

'Yeah. An older man.' Scandal dripped from Della's voice, humour too.

'A year older, if we're being technical.' Because, technically, Byrne gave the pyramids a run for their money, and Nova wasn't far behind. 'He's not exactly ancient.'

'A year's all it takes. Besides, Nova's not exactly living up to her age.' Della glanced again at the table where Nova was twirling her hair and making doe eyes at both boys.

Byrne ignored it, her attention on the boy in the shadows. 'We're halfway through the year; he'll graduate in a few months and when he does, there goes the prestige of dating a fifth year.'

'Oh, I know.' Della leaned in close, lowering her voice just a touch. 'But it's not the prestige of dating a fifth year Nova needs, she's got that in spades. What she needs, what she *wants*, is the legend; think of it, the pathos, the long kiss goodbye, him in his graduating gown, Nova in that red skirt she has in the back of her closet. The heels. The whole school will buzz with it for months after.'

Byrne eyed Della. 'What are you on about?'

Della smiled, and the expression lit up her face. 'Keeping Nova too busy with dark and brooding over there to fool around with magic.'

'She'll never go for him.'

'She will if you will.'

'Seriously?! You're going there?'

Della wiggled her brows, expression becoming devious. 'Seriously. Consider it as guiding Nova's choices without her thinking you're telling her what to do.'

'And you believe Nova is going to go for I guy I "like" just because?'

Della rolled her eyes. 'Is the sun a fusion reaction?'

Byrne narrowed her gaze, looking back to where Nova held court, magic a mirage sparkling around her fingers.

It could work, if only to force Nova to concentrate on a single target and shrink the audience exposed to her magic. And Della was right, it wouldn't take much to shift Nova's focus. All Byrne would have to do was sashay over there and start a conversation, and yet...

She shook her head. 'I don't like it.'

'What's not to like?'

'Romantic rivalry between siblings? Girls fighting over a guy? The manipulation? Take your pick.'

Della punched her arm. 'You are such a feminist; it's only a bit of fun.'

'It's a backhanded effort to control my sister, who, as arrogant and self-centred as she is, is still worth a *little* respect.'

'I thought she wasn't you sister?'

'You know what I mean.'

'No, I don't think I do.' Della stared at her, big brown eyes wide, her stupidly thick, mascara'd lashes sweeping downwards in a slow, deliberate blink.

The response forming on Byrne's tongue paused.

She considered Della, the gleam in her eye, the humour twisting her lips, and beneath it, the compassion. This wasn't a conversation about manipulating Nova; no, Della, the High Priestess, was manipulating someone else altogether.

Byrne scowled. 'Stop it.'

'Stop what?'

'Being the Priestess.'

Where the previous smile lit up her face, this one turned it from sly to the serenity of the Christian's Madonna. 'It's my job, sweetie.'

'Hmm.' Byrne burrowed into the chair, squirming until she could lay her cheek on Della's shoulder. 'Thank you.' The resentment in her middle was still there, but it no longer bit with the earlier ferocity. 'He is cute though.'

'Who?'

'The fifth year.'

'Oh? Maybe you should ask him out.'

'You think I need to be legendary? I mean, I don't think that skirt in Nova's closet is going to fit me, and you can forget about me wearing the heels.'

'I was thinking you need to have some fun.'

'I do have fun.'

'Hitting things and playing with your sword is *not* fun.'

'It's not a sword,' Byrne responded out of reflex. 'And sure, it's fun, keeps the spaghetti off my hips too, unlike your hair.'

This time Della's shot to the arm was a little harder.

'Ow!'

'My hips are fine.'

'Right, that's why you were complaining when you dragged me shopping last week.'

'Just because the fashion industry hasn't caught up with my glorious curves, doesn't mean there's anything wrong with them.'

'Whatever you say, High Priestess,' Byrne said, and laughed as Della launched another attack.

He looked up as laughter rang through the library. His eyes narrowed on the tussle going on in the corner. The two dark-haired girls, one brown-skinned, the other's complexion a pale gold, rolled about in the armchair, their laughter turning to giggles. The brown-skinned one was prettier, wide cheekbones, full lips, but it was the other that held his attention, made the darkness in his soul writhe.

The time was nearing. He'd made his plans, and soon the rest would play out as it was supposed to.

Chapter 4

'Hi, Betsy,' someone said from behind her.

Byrne didn't turn, and even though the sudden spurt of anger made her fingers fumble on the combination lock and making her miss the second key, she didn't let loose the snarl in her throat. She knew that voice – sweet and high and grating – the voice of an angel, her stepmother called it, or rather the voice of *her* angel. The little shit at Byrne's back hadn't been angelic from the moment she'd burst out of the womb. In fact, Byrne had spent half her life – after she'd stopped trying to actually like her little half-sister – convinced Rio was an agent of evil. A demoness.

The thought stuck with her, a pleasant half-second where fancy overtook reason and she imagined throwing Rio at the Horde. Would they take one look at her and run? All those horned and taloned monstrosities turning tail in the face of her half-sister's big round eyes, soft chin and sharp serpent tongue?

Byrne shook her head and spun the dial on her locker. No, with her luck the Horde'd shove a crown on Rio's head and fall at her delicate little feet in worship, and wouldn't that just be peachy.

But at least she'd get away with sticking Ahriman's blade in the little shit's gut.

The bright side. There was always one, right?

A sharp, pointed finger stabbed Byrne between her shoulders.

'Go away, Rio,' she said, and was proud the growl in her chest didn't make it past her throat.

Another sharp poke, harder than the first. And although it wasn't hard enough to shove her face into the thunder-cloud grey metal of her locker, Byrne's fingers still slipped on the lock dial, skidding past the first number in her combination.

Byrne spun about, the growl bursting through her self-restraint to twist her lips. 'I *said* fuc—'

The words died, impaled on her father's raised black brow. John Davin had a face like a slab of yellow-gold granite, all sharp sunken cheekbones and a jaw in a perpetual teeth-clenching frown. Despite the lines at the corners of his eyes, grey hadn't yet dared touch his hair, and his shoulders bowed to no one, least of all time.

His gaze, the same black-brown as her own, met hers. Byrne tried not to wilt, to force resolve and some of that anger back into her spine. It was a losing fight. Disapproval tightened her dad's shoulders under his white shirt, while disappointment shadowed the space between his eyes and deepened the creases at the corner of his mouth. Even though his hands were doubly hidden, once in the pockets of his dark grey trousers and twice by Rio standing between them with her triumphant smile, Byrne knew they'd be lightly clenched. It seemed like they always were.

And Rio... Byrne might have been looking at their dad, but she knew the little shit – a half-head shorter than Byrne and a full head shorter than their father – smirked. The expression would be curling the perfectly glossed bow of her lips and there'd be victory in those dark brown eyes.

Byrne hated her, hated her with all the darkness and all the passion that swirled safely under the membrane that separated her from her other self. Hated how cute Rio looked in the same school uniform that made Byrne a lumbering giant, hated the perfect white bow securing her chestnut-black ponytail, the way she folded her hands at her waist and how butter never looked like it'd melt in her mouth. But most of all, she hated the way their dad's eyes softened when they looked at the little shit, the way his jaw unclenched and he smiled.

Byrne hated Rio, and would do almost anything to turn that smile on herself.

And still... and still acid laced her voice when she spoke. 'Why are you here?'

Her dad's thick black brow twitched, a tiny movement, there and then gone.

Anger, Byrne thought.

No. Pain, Az said.

'You have an appointment,' he said. 'And your sister was kind enough to show me to your locker.' He said "kind" with particular emphasis, stressing the word with a glance at the top of the shit's head, the poufy rounded ears of her hair bow.

There was expectation in that look, a demand for Byrne to take the appropriate action. To show gratitude.

Byrne ignored it and turned back to her locker. No need to ask what the appointment was, there was only one appointment that necessitated parental escort and would draw her dad into the school before the final bell rang.

'I don't need an escort,' she said, spinning the locker combination.

'That is not what your sister says.'

The little shit was a tattletale, and the force of her smug little smile just about punched Byrne in the back. She didn't have to see it, she *knew* it was there.

'I'll get there on my own, Dad.' She jerked her locker open. 'I'm a big girl now, remember?'

A hand on her shoulder, her dad's big worn knuckles and calloused fingers at odds with his manicured nails and expensive suit. He dragged her around to face him, and she went reluctantly. Those serious brows and dark expectant eyes bore into Byrne, digging through her brain and skimming the membrane dividing her soul.

Underneath, Az sighed, sorrow and remembrance in the sound. *Father*, she said.

For a heartbeat, reality faded around Byrne. The hand clasping her shoulder wasn't her dad's worn and calloused one, but shone with golden rings, and the face staring back at her was longer, the nose straighter and sharper, and the eyes... The man's eyes shone like the sun, but the expression in them was the same, sombre and heavy with the weight of expectation, but there was something else too, something more that dulled the bright gold.

Before Byrne could grasp it, the memory-flash faded, leaving just her dad staring at her in the middle of the busy school corridor. For a moment, she thought she saw the same shadow in his eyes.

Sadness, Az whispered. *In all our lives, we pain our fathers.*

'I know,' her dad was saying, and Byrne scrambled to remember what he knew, what she'd said in the moments before the flash of ancient memory. 'But I'm going to take you anyway.'

The appointment. The big girl comment. Rio, the little shit, smirking in the background.

Byrne snatched her bag out of the locker and slammed the door.

She glared at her dad. 'Fine. Let's go.'

'And how did that make you feel?'

Like she wanted to punch the serene, interested expression struggling to cover up the harried look on the psychologist's face. Sure, the woman tried to hide it under discrete makeup and a double braid, but there were worry marks at the corners of the blue eyes and wisps of brown hair had long ago escaped the two neat plaits marching either side of her crown. And still...

And still Doctor Knowles, old enough to be her mum – her *real* mum – could pin Byrne to the back of the green armchair with its poufy cushions and high arms. The doctor would stare without seeming to stare and make her feel as if was she was actually peeling back the layers of her psyche to Az underneath.

Az, who watched. A dark presence lurking behind her eyes. Silent, always silent in these dreaded twice-weekly sessions.

If only Knowles actually *could* see Az, maybe then she'd believe. Maybe then the disbelief would vanish from the arch of her pale white forehead and the suspicion from her gaze.

If only.

Byrne turned away, stared out the window overlooking the postage stamp of white pebbles, one of those white snowman-like stone fountains at its centre.

'Byrne?' Knowles's low, soothing voice had an edge to it now. Not enough to cut, not yet. But soon it would if no answer was forthcoming.

She brought her attention back to the room, with its light scent of peppermint and lavender. Meant to soothe, Knowles had told her, meant to promote calm.

All it did was give her a headache.

'Angry,' Byrne said. Because that was what she was supposed to say, what Knowles and her father expected. Angry, she had anger issues and not a millennia-old bloodthirsty warrior lurking in the pit of her soul.

'Why were you angry?'

Because she had a millennia-old bloodthirsty warrior lurking in her soul. But she'd said that before, tried explaining about Az and Ahriman and the dreams, and seen only disappointment and then concern and fear. The first fear had been her step-mum's and then Rio's and finally her dad's. That'd hurt, that last one, the memory of his eyes widening, the pain flashing across his usually impassive brow, still stabbed her in the gut. Over and over and over.

At least Knowles knew how to keep her face blank. They must teach that at shrink school, *Dealing with Patients 101 – Turning your face to stone.*

'Byrne.' Knowles leaned forward in her chair, not the same type of green high-armed monstrosity that threatened to swallow Byrne whole, but a white one with a straighter back. 'We've been over this a number of times. You need to engage to get the most out of our sessions.'

'I am engaging.'

'No, you're phoning this in, telling me what I want to hear.'

Byrne shifted in the armchair, fighting the urge to cross her arms over her chest and stare out the window. 'Isn't that what you want?'

'No, I want you to get better, to deal with your anger, not push it down.'

'And telling you *why* I'm angry is supposed to do that, right?'

Knowles nodded. 'It's a start.'

'A start of what? Me not being angry?' Byrne snorted. 'Or were you hoping for inner peace or acceptance or, you know, not delusional?'

The doctor sat back, that stony, expressionless face becoming stonier, guarded, like her voice. 'I never said you were delusional.'

'But you think it. Everyone thinks it.' It was Byrne's turn to lean forward. 'Today I'm angry because Dad thought he had to give me an "escort" here, and because when he did, he brought Rio along and Rio thought it'd be funny to use her stupid little nickname – you know, "Betsy", the one she uses when she wants to call me a cow right in front of Dad's face. And I can't retaliate because Dad thinks it's just a cute nickname – a "pet name" he calls it, and doesn't Rio think that's a hoot. A "pet name" for her pet cow.'

Byrne pushed herself to the edge of the armchair, black school shoes thudding on the pale grey carpet. 'But that's not what really makes me angry. What *really* makes me angry is that no matter how many times I try to tell Dad or my step-mum what Rio's doing, they don't believe me because Rio's cute and sweet and not a backstabbing, vicious little shit, and I'm an angry delusional psycho.' Byrne stopped, breathing hard. 'No one *ever* believes me.'

Not her dad, not her friends. Not Nova.

Never Nova.

Not in all our lifetimes, Az whispered from the depths.

Memories hit Byrne between the eyes, flashes of light and colour, pain and screaming, so much screaming. In each one of them a battlefield full of demon corpses with Nova bloody and broken at its centre, barely hanging on to life while Della raised her arms to the sky and summoned power like lightning. And all because of one mistake, because Nova – or whatever she was called in that life – had trusted the wrong person, the betrayer.

Tellamoth.

It has to stop. Az pressed against the barrier between them, her urgency and determination seeping through the thin membrane, desperation an acidic aftertaste on the back of Byrne's tongue. *In this lifetime we have to make her listen, or...*

Or what? Byrne whispered back.

The dark-cold answered.

Byrne thumped back against the green cushions and shivered.

'It's not your sister you're upset with, is it?' Knowles's question brought Byrne back to the doctor.

Byrne stared at her and spent a moment trying to figure out which sister the doctor referred to, even as the cold-dark tip-toed through her bones. For a second, she saw the darkness – the soul-freezing cold – a spark of memory, barely enough to know what it was she felt, or experienced, barely enough to be called a *memory* and yet... Fear gripped her heart, flash-froze the muscle and stopped her lungs. Every thought, every sense, every molecule of her being screamed. If she'd had air, if she'd had muscles, she'd have screamed with them—

Knowles shifted, the movement breaking the memory.

The doctor must have taken Byrne's silence for some kind of answer. She was leaning forward in her chair again, scooting to the very edge of the seat, like those extra few centimetres made the metre and a half of empty carpet between them more intimate. And maybe it did, because the cold-dark retreated, sucked back into the pit with Az.

'It's not that your family don't believe you, Byrne. They're worried, and they want you to be well.'

'So, they sent me to you.' There should have been resentment in those words, but all her energy and emotion were gone, sapped by the cold and the dark, leaving... Nothing.

The doctor tilted her head, one of her ash-brown braids slipping off her shoulder. 'Isn't that what you would do if you were worried about your dad?'

Knowles tried to pin her with bright blue eyes, and Byrne... Byrne looked away, back out to the stone fountain in its sea of white. She'd been that fountain once, a serene stone in the midst of her neatly manicured life, there might have been weeds poking up between the pebbles but she'd been able to see everything, known who she was and where she was going, and now... Now she was still that stone, but there were cracks in the sides and the water bubbling up from within was just the overflow, the shadow before the cold, dark night.

She had to make Nova believe. She *had* to, and if she couldn't...

Deep inside, Az stirred. *We do what we have to.*

Chapter

The gym was silent save for the *shush* of her bare feet on the room's smooth parquet floor, its chill competing with the hot sweat running down her neck and pooling in the small of her back. She'd left the overhead fluoros off, and the only light came from the rising sun. It flooded through the big open doors to reception, barely reaching Byrne's dark, quiet corner.

In the half-light, the punching bag hanging in the corner was a demon – the long, black-vinyl cylinder a hulking monstrosity towering over her, its ram horns scoring the ceiling, the claws on the end of its long, heavily-muscled arms slashing at her face. With every blow of her fists against the thick, black armour growing out of its chest, new blood ran between her knuckles. Her blood and the demon's mixed in a thick, acidic mess – red into black, black into red. Where did she begin and it end? Was it Az? Was it the cold-dark? was it—

She twisted, spun, jumped, gloried in the sharp jolt, the heavy *thunk* as her heel smashed into the bag.

Twist again. Crouch. Spin. Foot sweeping under the bag. Missing the heady thud of impact but still moving. Stepping back, Ahriman a glimmer in her hands, half-there, half-not; difficult to tell if she was imagining the glaive with its curved blade and long metal haft, or if the weapon was actually there, forming out of the mists in defiance of the magic that kept it locked away. Whatever the thing in her hands, it was real enough to feel the weight of it, the runes carved in the shaft, the way they writhed against her skin.

Ahriman spun, backwards, forwards, a blur of motion, fending off imaginary monsters – the wicked curve of enemy swords, the clash of shields, the screech of talons. Again and again and again. Each impact shuddered up her arms, not enough to make the muscles scream. Not yet. Just enough to feel the burn, the way the bone moved, the pull of tendons. Magic of a different kind.

Lunge, thrust, parry, slash.

Az was there, in the pound of blood, the *smack* of her fists, the fire that consumed her knuckles, the sweat trickling down her spine. Patient, watching, waiting, guiding. A darkness living under her skin.

A demon charging from the left. Leap back, twist sideways, plant the back foot and brace. Ahriman's spiked end shoved deep into the ground, curved blade pointing up. Back straining, tendons standing out in collarbone and throat. Teeth gritted.

The shudder of impact, the demon impaled on Ahriman's blade.

Collapse her back leg, duck, spin. Leave the demon to flail about on Ahriman's tip as she came up underneath its guard. Summon the cold and dark swimming at her core, a new blade forming between her fingers, a thing of nothing and everything, screaming with the void. Thrust into the small chink between the demon's neck and shoulder, all the way to the knuckles, glory in the pump of ichor over her hand.

Victory.

She stepped back, panting. Looked at her hands.

No blood, no Ahriman, no blade made of the void. But the cold remained in her bones.

Clapping shattered the silence.

Byrne jerked upright, thrusting her hands behind her.

Ray stood with her shoulder propped against the wall, the gym manager a tall, lean shadow against the morning sun bleeding through the front windows. Her sleek brown hair with its long fringe and short back suited the angles and planes of the older woman's face; the stark, muscled lines of her body hidden for the moment under her black uniform.

'I love watching you train,' Ray said.

'I didn't know you where there.' Had her boss seen Ahriman? Had Byrne summoned the glaive this time, or was it still just Az, bringing the memory of the weapon to life in her hands? And what of the void-blade? Its chill sat in her bones and made her tendons ache.

'I figured that,' Ray said. She flipped the nearby switches, flooding the space with light. 'You didn't respond when I called your name.'

She'd been deeper in than she thought, letting Az slip through the membrane.

Byrne nodded, swallowed, wiped the sweat from her brow. 'Sorry. I guess I was in the zone.'

'It's all right.' Ray lifted a bottle. 'You could probably use this.'

The tall woman threw it, and for a second, as the red-filled plastic flew through the air, the overhead fluoros refracting through the liquid, Az rose in her blood, seized her muscles and—

Byrne snatched the sports drink out of the air, twisting the cap and taking a swallow in one smooth movement, even though her muscles clenched with the effort of pushing Az back, before she sliced the bottle to pieces.

'Thanks,' Byrne said.

'You're welcome.' Ray straightened, reaching behind to flip more light switches. 'I still don't get why you like to train in the dark.'

Because she could see the demons then. Not real ones, but memories of their foes. Could summon the images to her mind and bring a little bit of Az with them. It was the safest way to do so, maybe the only way to learn more about the other half of her soul, to get a grip on the power before it had a chance to overwhelm her.

She flexed her hand around the drink bottle, that creeping chill still in her tendons. The void-blade had been new, unexpected.

Byrne couldn't tell Ray that though, even if her boss would believe her. If it didn't get back to her dad, it might get Ray wondering why Byrne, regular high school kid, was fighting imaginary demons and from there... It was only a short hop and a jump to the psych ward.

Byrne shrugged. 'I just like it, helps me focus. Be zen and all that.'

Ray laughed, the sound as big and vibrant as the woman herself. 'Zen. I like that. I still think you'd do well to see Sensei Joan, take a couple of classes at the dojo.' She held up a hand before the objection had a chance to form on Byrne's tongue. 'Taking a couple of classes doesn't mean you have to spar, but it might clean up that sweep of yours. Looked a little messy. You should try shifting your weight over your toes, it'll help you transition to the kick.'

Byrne's mouth opened, then closed on the objection, even as Az, buried deep in the recesses of her mind, agreed about the sweep. She frowned. 'I'll think about it.'

Ray nodded. 'You do that. In the meantime.' She smiled and nodded towards the equipment room. 'Those weight machines aren't going to clean themselves.'

Rolling her eyes, Byrne chucked the empty Gatorade bottle in the recycling can. 'Yes, boss.'

Ray chuckled, tossing a spray bottle and rag at her. 'Go get 'em, girl.'

The sharp smell of anti-bacterial spray and the clink of weights followed her as she worked her way around the bench presses and pull-down machines. Byrne crouched to reach under the discs loaded onto the barbell on the squat press, spraying and wiping the white frame in an easy, practised motion.

When the gym was this quiet, cleaning the machines was almost a meditation; that's why she liked working Sundays. The morning crowd had come and gone after their fix of sweat and burn of muscle fibres, and there were still a few hours before the post-lunch rush desperate to work off that extra slice of cake. They'd spill through the doors and fill the gym with the pound of dance music and the thud of dumbbells.

There was nothing to worry about, no books to study, no sisters to fight, no—

'Hey.'

Byrne's head shot up, meeting the underside of a fifty-kilo weight disk with a loud clunk. 'Fu—'

There was a hand on her shoulder, another on the top of her head, guiding her out from under the squat press. 'Are you okay?'

'No.' She pushed the hand – large and long-fingered – off her head. 'I just cracked my head open.'

'Ooo-kay.' The grip on her shoulder fell away. 'Sorry.'

Still crouched, Byrne rubbed the offending spot. There was no blood, despite her scalp insisting it was split from crown to temple. She peered up to regard the voice at her side. She blinked, squinted against the light haloing the voice. It was a guy, that much she could tell, but the rest was obscured by the fluoro behind his head.

'Was there something you wanted?' she asked.

'Ugh, yeah.' His silhouette jerked a thumb over his shoulder. 'The manager said you could help me; I'm looking for a sparring partner.'

'For what? I say you got the whole sneaking up on people down pretty pat.'

'Hey, you were the one crouched under a loaded barbell.'

She scowled as she stood and wondered if the guy had purposefully positioned himself so the glare through the big front windows would blind her just as well as the fluoro. Maybe he was contemplating a career as a gunslinger and liked to strategically position himself so his opponents couldn't see his face. Whatever it was, she was getting sick of it.

'Whatever,' she said. 'Listen, we're a gym. If you're looking for a fight, or sparring partner or whatever, there's an Aikido dojo down the street.'

He leaned against the squat press's bare metal frame. 'Been there. Not my speed.'

Not his speed. If Byrne's head had rung a little less, she'd have rolled her eyes. Of course it wasn't his speed, because Sensei Joan demanded discipline and precision from her students and that was probably a little more than an adrenalin junkie could handle. *Hero.*

She picked up the rag and spray bottle at her feet and skirted around him, heading to the next workstation. It didn't hurt that she got a good look at him as she did, taking in the lithe physique, the strength in his slim shoulders hinted at by the way his t-shirt clung to the muscles underneath, and the cords in his pale, sun-kissed arms. Not the kind of musculature that came from lifting weights, at least not all of it.

Her gaze dropped to hands, taking in the rough, raised pads of flesh over his first two knuckles. Calluses, the kind gained from punching things with bare hands. Someone should tell him boxing gloves were a thing.

She dropped down beside the leg press, spraying and wiping in the same motion. 'There's the boxing gym in midtown.' The meatheads there liked whaling on each other a little too much for her taste, but she bet it would suit the hero. Spaghetti-string singlets and bare knuckles were in amongst that crowd.

Personally, she preferred it when her hands didn't look like bits of mangled meat, but then she also didn't go around hitting people in the face a lot, so there really wasn't much need for calluses to protect her hands. Demons didn't count as people, and even if they did... Well, mangled meat would be a pretty way to describe what their armour would do to her hands, calluses or no.

The boy crossed his arms, and she had to admit, it did nice things to his biceps, made the dark grey fabric of his tee strain around the muscle. 'Been there too. I'm looking for something with a little more... finesse.'

Finesse. That one got her looking up, all the way to his face, just to see if he was having her on. The lighting gods were still beaming down on him, but at least this time they weren't trying to blind her.

The hero was one of those pale, square-jawed, full-lipped individuals that belonged on the cover of a magazine or fronting a boy band. The white hair and dark brows were definitely boy band material, and she wondered, even as her pulse sped up and awkwardness set into her bones, if it was contacts making his eyes so blue.

She wasn't this shallow, she *wasn't*. A pretty face didn't mean shit, she knew that better than most. Pretty faces hid all sorts of sins, the kind that came with daggers in the dark and hallways lined with blood, screams and demons and betrayal.

At least his knuckles were ugly.

Byrne cleared her throat and stood, praying that the blush she could feel under her cheeks wasn't the blazing red she feared.

'Look,' she said or tried to. The blush on her cheeks had worked its way into her voice, and made it croak. Damn the hormones that turned her brain to mush. What was the use of them anyway? Other than to the embarrass the shit out her. She cleared her throat and tried again. 'Maybe you better tell me *exactly* what you're looking for.'

His arms remained crossed, and really, that t-shirt should be banned or something, 'cause with the way he leaned against the press, it rode up his sides and... Yeah. She saw half-naked guys all the time, all sweaty and glistening under the gym lights, such a small slice of barely-tanned skin shouldn't get her heart racing, not matter how ripped it was.

She forced her eyes upwards.

His glacial blue ones were narrowed.

'I'm *looking*,' he said, putting a little extra emphasis, if not quite a sneer on the last word. 'For someone who knows how to fight, and not the ritualised shit they do at the dojo, or the bloodsport in midtown. Normally, I'd go for the local MMA club but this town doesn't have one, and when I asked around...' He gestured with both hands at Byrne. 'I was told to speak to you.'

She was gonna kill someone, probably Ray.

A glance over the hero's shoulder and— Yeah, there was the gym manager looking up over the reception counter, a grin on her tanned face, wriggling her eyebrows and giving her the thumbs up.

Ray was always trying to get her to re-join the dojo, to "interact" like she used to before she'd thrown a fellow Aikido student into a wall and almost stomped on his face.

Normally, the separation between Az and her – the regular, old everyday Byrne with a closet full of anime tees and denim, who went to school and struggled with quadratic equations – was clear. But when she was on the floor, her adrenalin up, Az slipped through, rode in on the pound of her heart and the *thunk* of fists into the bag.

It was hard to keep Az under control, and Az... Asenath Uthor, the Empire's Sword, didn't spar – for her, holding back was death. And the longer this war with the Horde went on, the harder it was to keep the Sword under control. Not because Byrne couldn't, but because she didn't want to.

So no, Byrne didn't spar, not with anyone with bones to break or flesh to bleed. Not with Sensei Joan, not the with meatheads in midtown and certainly not with the pretty, white-haired, K-Pop star wannabe in front of her.

'I don't spar,' was what she meant to say, what was on the tip of her brain, but what came off her tongue was, 'Six am. Here. I'll let you in.'

Nova

Chapter

Six am. Shit. She'd actually said it. Those words had come out her mouth and the cute hero had nodded, kinda almost smiled around his scowl, and said 'Sure, six am. Don't be late.'

Don't be late.

That had been yesterday, and almost a day and a half later the memory still made her mad.

She snarled and kicked a stone off the path, imagining it was the hero's head. It bounced off the pale trunk of a birch tree and rolled into the leaf litter under the little forest on either side of the bike track. Birds cawed, occasionally darting across the bright blue sky, the warm afternoon sun casting their long shadows on the pale orange dirt. In the distance, beyond the birches *shushing* leaves and her black Mary Janes *crunching* the path, traffic roared on Port Wyden's main drag.

Don't be late. The hero's words repeated in her brain.

She wasn't quite sure what pissed her off more, the hormones that had hijacked her tongue or his last words. As if he was doing her a favour. He hadn't even given his name, and her stupid hormones had obviously robbed her brain of the ability to function.

She should let Az have him, pound his face into mush. If she concentrated enough, Byrne could probably pull her other half back just long enough to stop before she killed him. Maybe. Possibly.

Probably not.

'Shit,' she said, and kicked another stone.

'What's got your knickers in a twist?'

Byrne jumped, heart pounding, the tell-tale prickle of magic teasing her fingers as Ahriman began to form.

The voice had come out of thin air, the speaker's breath brushing her ear.

The empty space to her right shimmered and parted around a girl, a little younger, an inch taller, midnight hair flowing straight and true to her hips, amber eyes shining with amusement. Everything about her was perfect, from her smooth, pale-gold complexion to the drape of her navy school sweater and her bleach-white knee-high socks, without the slight speck of dirt or wrinkle.

Byrne's heart settled back in her chest, the tingle of magic fading from her fingers. 'Nova,' she said, annoyance mixing with relief in her voice. 'You scared me.'

Her sister from a different lifetime smiled, the expression radiant, compelling. If Byrne hadn't known better, couldn't see the tell-tale shimmer of power around Nova's shoulders, she'd be sucked in by that smile. Would do anything to make sure Nova never stopped.

'You should pay more attention,' Nova said.

'You should stop using magic in the street.'

Nova's smile faltered a little, a tiny downturn at the corners, the sourness of the old argument taking the glimmer out of the air. 'Don't tell me what to do, Byrne. You're not my sister anymore.'

That stung. Byrne should be used to it, should be able to shrug off the barb, but no matter how many times it was thrown, it always found a way beneath her skin. Instead, she scowled and wrapped her hands around the straps of her school backpack.

'You're putting the rest of us at risk.'

'You can handle it,' Nova retorted, turning her back and walking down the path.

Nova wore arrogance the same way she wore perfume and expertly applied her makeup. Just enough to accentuate the depth of her eyes, the curve of her lip, the line of her cheekbones but not enough to incur the wrath of the teachers.

Byrne watched her go, Nova's head high, her shoulders straight, like the books straining at the edges of her school bag didn't weigh a thing, and for a second... For a second the dirt path winding through a carefully tended copse was a wide marble hallway and the thin-trunked trees where supplicants, bowing in Nova's wake.

On the tail of that memory came another, not as ancient but just as alien. In it, she stood in a crumbling doorway, Ahriman swinging before her, filling a stone hallway with demon corpses. Behind Byrne, Nova – with a different name, a different face but her eyes still burning like the sun – drove a knife between her own ribs, committing them to another turn of Life's Wheel and another reincarnation, uncaring of the villagers dying in the square. The ones they could have saved.

'Do you even care?' The words burst out of Byrne, coming from the place deep in her soul that remembered the pound of her heart and the sick feeling in her chest as the villagers screamed.

Nova stopped and turned, confusion lining her face. 'What do you mean?'

'Care. Do you even care about us, about school, the boys, our parents or is all of this...' Byrne gestured to the sun pendant half-seen through the open collar of Nova's shirt, the fiery orange quartz half encased in a delicate gold filigree.

Byrne gripped her own pendant – the slim, upside-down crescent of milky stone wrapped in the middle with tarnished silver. Each a symbol of their other selves and the centuries of history that only she remembered. The terrifying, almost prophetic slivers of past lives that haunted her nightmares, promising the carnage and pain to come.

Unless we stop it, Az whispered.

Byrne gripped her pendant, as always, unsure if she wanted to hold it tighter or rip it away.

Nova cocked her head, a glitter, like ice, forming in her gaze. 'Is all of this what, Byrne?'

She should be scared of that glitter, the sensible part of her knew that, but the sensible part was tired, worn down by nightmares and the constant battle with Az and the darkness. There was only pain and anger left. That, and desperation.

'Is all of this just some kind of ego trip?' she said. 'The great Empress Nova trying to reclaim the Universe, and stopping the Horde is just a side benefit. Screw the world, the people who are going to die under their claws, just so long as you get what you want.'

Nova blinked, those great amber eyes blank for a moment before filling with anger. She was in Byrne's face in the next breath, crossing the meters of dirt between them like it was nothing.

'You think I want this?' Nova growled the words. 'You think I want to spend my life fighting monsters from another dimension, or worrying about when the next Reaper is going to come after my mum?'

Byrne opened her mouth to argue, but Nova cut her off. 'Maybe you think that I like watching my friends bleed? Perhaps you thought I got a laugh out of it when that archdemon threw you off the lighthouse and we spent an entire week looking for you? Do you think it was easy lying to your dad about where you were, or that I slept like a baby thinking you were *dead*?'

Nova paused, her breathing coming hard, and Byrne spoke into it. 'I don't know, Nova. It's pretty hard to tell when you're throwing your magic around like you're daring the Horde to find you, and for what? Sneaking up on me and seducing a couple of boys you don't even care about?'

Nova stepped back. Fury tightened her jaw, compressed her lips and turned her skin a lighter shade of gold. 'I have my reasons.'

Byrne covered the distance Nova put between them, taking it in one big stride. 'What are they?'

'They're my reasons, and you need to trust me.'

'Because you're the Empress? I don't think so.'

'Trust me because I was your sister.'

And there it was a second time, the barb finding its mark. Byrne snarled. 'But you're not anymore.'

The anger in Nova's eyes dimmed and something else took its place, something that tried to curl around the hurt in the Byrne's chest and replace it with... fear?

She shook it off, and now it was her turn to step back, away from Nova's influence and the shimmer of her magic.

Nova was quicker; she grabbed Byrne's hand and sandwiched it between her own. 'Trust me, Az. Like you used to, when we were kids.'

Az. The nickname rang in her head, reached down into the darkness, seeking the other presence and when it found her... Memories, ancient and fragmented rose from the depths of her being, of the two of them running through gold-lined hallways the width of a highway, of ceilings carved with the history of the Universe, of sneaking into the grand audience chamber and hiding behind the statues of rulers past. Of dancing across that same chamber, packed with courtiers, feeling her sister's magic around her, hiding her, and knowing Nova would keep her safe.

'Trust me.' Nova took her other hand, and now Byrne could see the other emotion behind the anger in Nova's eyes, could name it, even as it chilled the fury in her heart.

Desperation.

'Please, Az, I need you to believe in me, to be the Sword at my back. I can't do what I need to without you, I never could.'

Byrne was nodding, was falling into Nova's big amber eyes. She'd do anything to erase the terrible loneliness there, would rip a hole in the fabric of the Universe and take on the Demon Lord itself to lift the burden from Nova's hands... Hands that held hers with such fervour, hands that glowed—

Byrne jerked out of Nova's grip, almost stumbling in her haste to put distance between them. 'You're using magic on me?' Was it hurt or just shock that made her voice high and pinched her heart?

Nova reached out, that pleading and desperation still in her eyes. 'Az—'

'No.' She held up a hand, taking another step back. 'No, you don't get to call me that. Only my sisters call me that, and we're not sisters anymore, remember? Or are you just making an exception for the moment, so you can manipulate me into looking the other way while you bring hell down on us?'

Nova's face went hard, eyes turning to stone, determination washing away all other emotion. 'You don't know a thing about it, Byrne, don't care what I've had to do to keep the Horde at bay.'

Byrne scoffed. 'Don't tell me about what you've had to do because I remember what you've done. I'm the only one who remembers.'

'So you say, but where's the proof?' Nova advanced, and maybe it was the anger rolling off her in waves, or maybe it was the Empress bleeding through Nova's skin, but she seemed to get taller, until she blotted out the sun. 'None of the rest remember anything, all we know is what the medallions have shown us. Snatches of memory and none of it like what you say happened.' Nova loomed over her. 'What makes you so special, Byrne? Why should I trust you when you won't return the favour?'

Nova's every word, backed by her magic, cut at Byrne. Small cuts and big, slicing deeper, thrusting harder, seeking out the tender bits in her heart, her confidence. Her soul. She felt herself shrinking, her knees begging to kneel and prostrate herself before

Nova's radiance. Her tendons were weak, muscles trembling and her joints were bending, the ground getting closer—

Cold streamed through Byrnes bones, slipping past Az, clawing at the membrane between them.

Byrne snarled. 'Because I know. I remember. And every lifetime, every go at the Wheel, you make the. Same. Mistake.' She spat the last word.

'I'm not going to fall in love with Tellamoth.'

'How would you know? We don't even know what he looks like.'

'Which is convenient, don't you think? Of all the things you recall, Tellamoth isn't one of them.'

'Because he looks different. *Every* time. A different face, a different name but always the same goal. Get into your heart and drive a stake through it.'

'So, I'm supposed to be a stone? To just carve my heart out and not care about anyone?'

'No, I just…' Byrne gripped her head. Maybe if she pressed hard enough, she could squeeze the answer out. 'I don't know, I just know that the more you throw your powers about, the more the Empress rises and the more you glow. Glow, Nova. Not in a dewy, flushed cheeks way, but radiant, and the more you do that, the faster the Horde – the faster Tellamoth – will find you.'

Nova leaned in close, her expression softening. 'Byrne, as much as we fight, I still listen to you, and no matter his face, Tellamoth isn't going to get me this time.' She gripped Byrne's shoulders, and this time the warmth flowing between them had nothing to do with magic and everything with the two little girls hiding in the audience chamber. 'I promise.'

For a second, Byrne let herself believe, let the glow of a half-forgotten childhood sweep away the dread certainty swirling in her gut. 'I just... There's something coming, Nova. Something new, worse than what we've faced before. I feel it.' She pressed a fist to her stomach. 'Right here, where the Sword lives.

Sometimes I think I dream it.'

'What is it?'

'I don't know, I just know I need time.'

'For what? A plan?'

'I don't...' She growled. 'It's in my head somewhere. I just need a little more time, some breathing room to dig it out and prepare.'

'That's it? You need time?' Incredulity threaded Nova's voice, lifted her brows and filled her expression with questions. 'The Horde's already here Byrne, we don't have time; the veil between our dimensions is getting thinner; Suun still hasn't figured out where the actual breech is and Fion—' She broke off mid-sentence.

'Fion... what?'

Nova shook her head. 'Let it go, Byrne. The point is, we've had all the time we're gonna get and the only thing keeping the Horde back now, is us. We need the Empress and her power to close the gate.'

'But we haven't found—'

Nova held her hand up, and Byrne stopped as if she'd hit a wall. In the depths of Nova's eyes, power swirled, the power of a sun. The power of the Empress, ruler of the Universe. 'I'll be ready when we do. In the meantime...' She lifted her chin, somehow straightened beyond the five and half feet of her natural height. 'Do your duty, Sword Uthor. Watch my back as you have sworn, in this life and all the others.'

Power splashed against Byrne's mind, the radiant glow of the sun slipping under her skin, hissing against the darkness in her middle. It boomed in her ear, demanding compliance, reaching deep inside to pull the other, the Sword from the darkness. She came in a rush, bursting past Byrne the girl, a maelstrom of blood and violence, of duty and honour.

Byrne fought her for a second, but the ancient half of her soul slapped her down – a child before a god.

'Yes, Empress. I am yours.'

Behind Nova, the Empress smiled. 'Good.'

Chapter 7

'They're coming through the gates!'

Az yanked Ahriman out of the solider-demon's guts, spraying ichor and innards across the white-gold floor. The monster collapsed, armoured knees hitting marble, swaying as it tried to hold the pale ropes of its intestines in with thick, clawed hands. It toppled, a grey, red-striped tree joining the rest of its kin in a forest of eyeless heads and curved horns.

The Great Hall was resplendent with blood. The colonnades rising to domed arches splashed with the bright red of the courtiers who hadn't run fast enough, the guards caught unawares. Across the marble floor, black blood ate into the intricate inlay of gold and stone, mixing with the vibrant silks and precious gems of nobles and demons alike. Instead of the ring of conversation, the sharp fizz of hundred-year-old champagne and the strains of the orchestra – their chairs and instruments abandoned in the first terror-filled moments of the battle – there was the whine of pulse rifles, the clash of nano-steel on horn and the harsh, guttural cries of the Horde.

Az spun, Ahriman a dance of golden metal in her hand, impaling the solider-demon creeping up behind, but not before it landed a bloody slash across her arm.

Pain radiated from the long, ragged tears in the delicate

armour and the larger wound in her side. The black silk and silver nano-mail of her ceremonial robes had been no match for the long fight, although the ornate, interlocking leaves of her chest-plate had done their job. At least she'd managed to ditch the long, leg-tangling skirts after the ceremony. At the time, the freedom of movement and Majordomo's scowling face as she'd strode out in the thigh-length tunic and tabard, legs clad in black nano-mail and boots, had been justification enough to ignore protocol, but now... She spun again, taking another demon that had worked its way in behind her.

Now she wished she'd heeded the niggling doubt in her middle. Now she wished she'd *made* Jaya listen, or taken control of the palace herself. A bloodless coup and a traitor's death would have been better than this.

What should have been a wedding was a massacre.

She wanted to ask how the fuck a full company of Horde had breached the capital's defences, let alone the palace, but the sick feeling in the pit of her soul suggested she already knew.

Too fast, it was all happening too fast.

'General Uthor!' The commander on the other side of the massive hall spoke behind her ear, his words relayed by the comm implanted in her skull. Even with a hundred metres of carnage between them, he looked tired, his golden chest-plate and greaves showing scars of battle, while the skirt of his white tabard with its golden embroidery was scorched and torn.

She didn't know his name, but he hadn't been a commander at the start of the night; Captain Szilágyi lay somewhere in the mess of bodies beyond the delicate latticework of the great doors, closed in that first panic-filled rush of violence.

'Your orders?' he asked. The tiredness and hopelessness in his shoulders didn't make it to his voice.

Run, she wanted to yell. Save yourselves and leave us to drown in our own royal blood. But the words wouldn't come, held back by duty and guilt.

'Close the inner doors.' She didn't raise her voice but it boomed nonetheless, amplified by the torc wrapped around her neck and relayed across the battlefield.

'But General, the citizens—'

'Are lost, Commander.' Out beyond the Palace's defence barrier, all was lost. The gleaming skyscrapers, the magnificent gardens strung like jewels between suburbs that reached for the sky, all of it lost. A millennia to build an empire, an hour to lose it.

'Close the inner doors,' she said. 'Have the rest of the Imperial Battalion hold the Hall.'

Across the other side of the hall, with a hundred and thirteen metres of marble between them, she saw the small man nod. 'We'll hold to the last.'

'No,' she said, already turning, feeling the wound in her side, the ache of the energy blast her armour hadn't stopped, the blood that had saturated the black robes before the medbots took hold. This, at least, she could do for her people. 'Hold until my signal, then get the survivors out.'

'What signal?'

'You'll know it.' It would blaze through the Universe, impossible to miss. And maybe, just maybe it would come in time to save the few who remained. The ones who weren't already screaming.

'Yes, sir. Until I see the signal.'

She nodded and ran.

Carnage hadn't made it this deep into the palace, hadn't stained the pillars red or rent the luminescent white latticework on the walls. There was no stench of burning flesh, no ichor eating at the marble floors nor brightly clad bodies thrown against the walls or slumped in the little fountains where palace hallways met. There was sound though, the rhythmic boom of the cannons, the distant whine of laser fire, the screaming… All of it heard over the harsh rasp of air in her lungs, the desperate pound of her boots.

The screaming would chase her through the lives to come, would haunt her dreams just like the dark, deadly knowledge in her gut. But only if she reached Mur in time, only if they completed the ritual.

She ran on, boots ringing on the hard floor.

There was fighting up ahead, the pulse of energy weapons, the ringing clash of blades, the blood-curdling war cry of the Executioner.

Az put on another burst of speed, vision streaking as the extra effort pumped the blood out the wound in her ribs faster, even as she willed her neuro-pharm into action. Felt the warmth of adrenalin spreading through her system, the chill buzz of another load of medbots rushing to stem the tide of blood from her side.

Security footage flashed across her visor, showing empty corridor after empty corridor. Where was the battle? Where was the Empress? Where were the guards?

'Helix! What's wrong with security?'

The cool voice of the palace AI answered. 'Security is functioning within parameters.'

She grunted, saving her breath for running. If that was true, her visor would be red with the gun turrets tracking her every move. Instead, there were delicate holo-paintings playing where the emergency exit lights should be, and her visor showed nothing more than empty hallways.

Security had been hacked.

She didn't swear, there was no time to swear; the Imperial suite was ahead. Az slowed, wishing she had a drone, or anything to throw into the air and send around the corner ahead. A gun-hover would have been nice, a little ball of death to take out the combatants she could hear the other side of the junction. A pistol even. She held out her hand and summoned Ahriman, the glaive's elaborately carved golden haft a comforting weight.

Another cry, high-pitched, agonised. Dying. Gods, don't let it be Marzanna.

A deep breath, a glance around the corner. A graveyard of demons, black armour scattered over the floor, a lake of demon blood eating into the marble, limbs and heads and horns, the beady stare of sightless eyes, and above it all the Executioner. Marzanna was a whirling dervish, screaming as she lay down death, the twin flashes of her blades singing their own song.

The last demon dropped.

Marzanna fell silent, her blades at her side.

Carefully, Ahriman held upright at her side, her other hand out, Az stepped around the corner.

'Marzanna.'

The woman looked up, the ivory skin of her face flushed, strands of hair that had escaped the intricate braids of her dark-blonde mohawk, stuck to her cheek. The red silk of her dress uniform was stained black with demon blood, the ebony lacework of the armour covering her chest and shoulders slick with the same, making it impossible to tell if any of the gashes on her arms and torso bled. But it wasn't the possibility of the Empress's left hand dying from blood loss that made Az's heart clench, it was the rage and madness swimming in the depths of her gaze, the way Marzanna's green eyes looked through Az like she wasn't there.

One careful step in front of the other, Az advanced. 'Marzanna, talk to me.'

'They're dead.' Marzanna's normally smooth voice was broken and cracked, a sure sign she'd been screaming warcries for a while.

'They are. You killed them.' Although whether Marzanna referred to the demons or the Imperial guards mixed in with the corpses, Az didn't know. Both, perhaps.

Another step and another. She might not be in striking range of Marzanna's blades yet, but the woman known as the

Executioner could throw them with the same accuracy with which she could stab them into a person's gut. And from the looks of the severed arm in the white of the Imperial uniform – the cut too clean to be the work of a being with talons – the Executioner had lost her last hold on reality.

The Executioner was likely to kill friend as foe.

Grip tightening on Ahriman's haft, ready to bring the weapon around at the first sign of aggression, willing the meds in her bloodstream to move faster, Az sidled closer. 'Marzanna, where's the Empress?'

'...killed them. I killed them.' Marzanna lifted a blade, the edge dripping blood, black and red mixed together.

Az tensed, but Marzanna was looking beyond her, the tip of her blade pointed at the space just over Az's shoulder.

'They tore through the Universe,' Marzanna said. 'Split apart reality and flooded through. Horns and talons, endless. The red sun behind them...'

The blade dropped, Marzanna's arm going limp, the animation draining from her body.

The fugue, a brief moment where the madness let go. It wouldn't last long and Az didn't waste the opportunity, rushing forward—

A blade, the acidic old meat stench of demon rising off the edge, hovering millimetres from Az's throat.

'Marzanna.' Az swallowed, trying to find moisture in a suddenly dry mouth. 'The Empress is in danger. Let me through.'

The blade shifted, the flat of it catching Az's jaw, pressing until she turned her head.

Marzanna's forest green eyes met hers, clear, hard. Focussed. The fog of insanity lifted. 'The Universe, Az, the demons tore through it.'

For a second, caught in Marzanna's eyes, she saw what Marzanna had seen; the shimmer in the air, a mirage becoming a rainbow before it split down the middle and a darkness with talons and teeth spilled through. It filled the hallway, not just with soldier demons but the red haze of another sun, the stench of death.

She knew what that was, recognised the waves in the air, the way the fabric of reality seemed to gather in invisible hands like some kind of curtain. It was a portal, an impossibility of magic and tech designed to reach between Universes and connect realities that should never touch. It was a gate that didn't respect reality much less petty things like orbital defence grids and nanosteel.

Marzanna's blade disappeared from her neck,

A chill formed in Az's gut. 'The walls won't hold them,' she whispered. She turned to the doors behind Marzanna. A meter of solid nanosteel shielded by biogrids and lasers, and it might as well have been straw.

She was over the bodies before the chill found her heart. She plunged her hand through the hologram concealing the security pad. The sharp bite of the biogrid testing her DNA barely registered on her brain, there was only the pound of her heart and that icy fear whispering *hurry, hurry, hurry*.

Locks *thunked*, the door shimmered as the energy shield died and the great round slab of elaborately carved nanosteel rolled aside.

Az was into the antechamber, staring down the throat of an open portal. The red, sulphur-heavy miasma of the Horde poured through the side of the rift facing Az, even as soldier demons poured through the other, like two doors sliced into paper-thin space.

Ahriman swept up and out, tearing through an emerging soldier demon before it had a chance to turn.

There was another and another after that. Az never stopped moving, Ahriman a storm of sunmetal in her hands, while Marzanna was a tornado of fury and death at her side. Demons died. The antechamber became a mound of hard-shelled corpses, and still they came on.

A talon got through Az's guard, and agony exploded as it ripped a new gash in her back. A hand on her shoulder – human, warm – yanking her backwards, a sword deflecting another claw meant for her throat.

She stumbled out of the antechamber into the room beyond. Marzanna was still in the thick of it, her blades twin arcs of lightning amidst the never-ending horns and talons coming through the rip in reality. They couldn't win this fight, couldn't close the portal, not by themselves, and there were more important things now.

The cold in her gut whispered *hurry, hurry, hurry*.

'Marzanna, retreat!' She yelled it as loud as she could, hoping, praying that the other woman wasn't yet too far gone—

Marzanna leapt, a magnificent backwards arch, her blades still flashing, carving up demon armour and limbs.

Az struck – fist punching through the illusion over the antechamber's security door, the biogrid no longer a bite but a painful, skin-searing burn assessing her DNA – and hit the emergency lock.

Marzanna barely cleared the threshold before the bulkhead slammed home.

Az didn't wait to see what happened next. The gun turrets that had activated when she hit the lock would tear the demons inside the antechamber to pieces, but they wouldn't stop the flow, and the bulkhead itself... How long until whatever force controlled the portal simply opened another?

She ran deeper into the Imperial suite, pain rocking her body. Marzanna at her side for a few strides before streaking ahead.

Beyond the antechamber, the suite was a jumble of broken furniture and carbon scoring, the ruins of a gun-hover jerking and shuddering on the ground, the antique rug underneath starting to smoulder as sparks of energy set it alight. Az ran, following Marzanna over more guards, slamming into inner doors, not as thick as the antechamber's bulkheads, not meant to stop an attack.

And then Az was bursting over the threshold, Ahriman humming in both hands, her HUD taking in the scene. Four Mammoth demons, backs laden with human-sized generators, their tree-trunk legs braced as they aimed massive energy blasters at a thin yellow-red energy shield.

Huge streams of power punched the shield, the thin half-sphere rippling under the assault, while inside...

There was Mur, the High Priestess with her arms spread wide, strain warring with concentration on her dark mahogany face, tattoos blazing as she held the shield against the Mammoth demons' guns. The long panels of her azure robes were stained with blood and at her feet... The chill in Az's gut solidified into a dagger of dread.

The Empress lay at Mur's feet, blood saturated the white and gold of her elaborate wedding gown, a tide of it spilling from a wound in her chest, soaking the golden peacock feathers red. More blood stained her teeth, spilled over her chin and stuck long, inky strands of hair to her face. Medea, the Empress's sister and Imperial Heir, knelt at her side, healing magic spilling from her hands, but even from where Az stood, with four demons and a half dozen metres between them, Az knew it wouldn't be enough.

There was no more time.

Az redlined her neuro-pharm. Warnings blazed across her HUD even as chemicals flooded her bloodstream. Time slowed, Az felt nothing. No fear, no rage, no pain, only a dead calm certainty.

She flowed into battle, half woman, half machine. Ichor flew, black acidic sprays of demon blood hitting Az's armour, the thin shield bubbling and buzzing. The greaves covering her arms smoked where the shield failed. Ahriman spun and stabbed, light as air, an extension of herself.

The first Mammoth fell.

Distantly, she heard Marzanna scream, saw the Executioner's blades as slow-motion lightning in the corner of her vision.

A second Mammoth on the ground, chest-sized head separated from its body.

The third died, and Az realised she'd lost some time somewhere, that she couldn't remember what happened between the first demon and the one still twitching at her feet. But it didn't matter, 'cause there was still one more to go, and the High Priestess's shield was buckling.

She and Marzanna attacked it in unison, the Executioner going for the weak spot behind its armoured knees, while Az leapt, sinking everything she had into a strike at its neck.

Ahriman sank deep, twisted and caught. Blood poured from the wound, but the beast wasn't dead. Marzanna jumped.

The Mammoth's head joined the others on the antique rugs.

The shield around the Empress collapsed, the High Priestess with it.

Az caught Mur before she hit the floor.

Exhaustion lined every part of her best friend's face and her huge azure eyes drifted shut.

Az shook her, a sharp, violent movement. 'There's no time, Mur. We need to do the Ritual.'

Mur barely stirred.

Az slapped her.

Mur gasped and jerked upright, out of Az's grip.

'The Ritual.' Az was in her face, eye-to-eye, nose-to-nose. 'Now, Mur, before we lose everything.'

'Oh, I think that time has come and gone,' said a familiar, honey-smooth voice from behind.

Az spun, time still moving slow, allowing her to take in the new portal, and the tall man standing before it. The normally strong planes of his face were gaunt, the cloud-white hair snarled and singed, like the once-fine black suit hanging in tattered rags on his equally gaunt body.

He stared at her, blue eyes dark with emotions she didn't want to face.

'Tellamoth.'

Tellamoth.

Byrne jerked upright, the dove-grey bed covers pooling around her waist, sweat sticking her nightie to her back. Fairy lights twinkled in the gauzy white canopy above her head, competing with the morning light spilling across her feet, the warm yellow turned pale pink by the filmy curtains. Somewhere distant, crockery clinked and steam *zhushed* into milk, while the dark scent of coffee teased her nose, but Byrne ignored it. Her eyes were still focussed on the gaunt face, the matted white hair, even as the rest of the dream shredded, leaving the sharp point of dread behind.

Tellamoth.

And then, like an echo of the dream, a honey-smooth voice whispering in her ear, *Remember me.*

Her legs were boiling. She threw the covers off, swung herself around until they were dangling off the bed and—

Remember me, the voice whispered again.

Remember what? Remember who? Head in her hands she tried to catch the rest of the dream, tried to recall the images, the names, the places. But all she captured was urgency and pain, the frantic rush to... to...

Damn it! Why couldn't she remember?

'Byrne?' A hand on her back.

She was out of the bed, spinning into the centre of the room, away from the door where she had space to move. Her hand was out and she was pulling the magic from her gut, remembering the feel of Ahriman's heavily carved haft as the weapon materialised—

She looked down... There was nothing there, just her outstretched arm, fingers curled as if to grip something, and on her feet... She scrunched her toes, feeling not the hard soles of armour-reinforced boots but the thick pile of the circular rug in the middle of her room.

She shook her head, trying to figure out... What was she trying to figure out?

'Byrne?'

She looked up.

Della stood between Byrne and the door, worry creasing her brow. Her dark brown hair was tied back in high ponytail and she wore a navy sweater over her white school shirt and plaid skirt. There was a school bag by the doorjamb, plopped in the middle of the threshold like it had been dropped, like it's owner had rushed across the minefield of clothes and books littering Byrne's bedroom floor.

'Byrne,' Della said again, and there was something in her voice, a sternness that went beyond the natural tones of a teenager, spoke of power and command. It caught Byrne under the chin, turned her attention to Della's dark steady gaze. 'Bad dream?'

She nodded. The echoes of it rang in her head; the roar of monsters piercing her ears, the afterimage of blood and bone spraying across her face—

Byrne shook it away, stumbled a few steps away from the bed and Della, and collapsed in the chair in front of the desk.

'Want to talk about it?' Della asked.

'I...' Byrne blinked, focussed on the Della, now sitting on the

side of her bed. Not a sign of blood or bone to be found and yet...
'I don't remember it.'

Della cocked her head, one dark brow arching. 'Are you sure?'

She nodded, and then just as quickly shook her head.

'It was one of *those* dreams, wasn't it?'

'Yeah.'

'Which one of us died this time?'

Byrne scrubbed her face. 'No one, I think. I mean, I didn't really *see* anyone die, but there was so much bloo—' Bile rose in her throat. She pressed her hand to her mouth and ran for the bathroom. Out the bedroom door, down the long hall with its wall of glass facing the inner courtyard, her bare feet *thwaping* on the polished wood. Then she was pushing past her little sister, elbowing Rio out of the way as she reached for the bathroom door, ignoring the shout from behind that sounded like her step-mum. She didn't even slam the bathroom door closed before she was kneeling in front of the toilet, the tiny hexagon tiles cold under her knees, spewing the memory of blood and guts into the bowl.

She heaved and then heaved again, nothing coming out but bile and the orange, carrot-fleck bits of stuff, trying to erase the memory of all that red.

'Byrne, honey?' Her step-mum's voice came from the doorway, concern making it high and soft.

'It's okay, Mrs Davin.' Della. Byrne couldn't see her, not with her head still in the white porcelain bowl, but she could picture her friend sliding by Kokoro, a gentle hand on her step-mum's shoulder as she pushed her out of the bathroom. 'I'll take care of it.'

The gentle *clunk* of the bathroom door closing, the *snick* of the lock, the *clack* of Della's shoes on the tiles, then she was kneeling beside Byrne, warm hand on her shoulder as the other pulled the hair back from her face. And still, all Byrne saw was the blood—

She heaved again.

'That's good, get it all out; all those memories, all that badness.' Della's hand shifted to her back, and now there was more than just body-warmth radiating from it. The shiver of power, the soul-deep energy of the High Priestess seeped through Byrne's spine, reaching deep inside. It grabbed hold of the sick, the wash of red and... It was gone. Dissolved to not even a memory.

Relief swept the adrenalin from Byrne's veins, left warmth and the euphoric buzz of endorphins behind. She blinked away tears as she pushed back from the toilet and sat on her heels. She stared without seeing at the column of family photos on the wall above the cistern, standing out from the emerald tiles in their golden frames.

Gradually, the floor under her knees and chill of the sweat-damp nightie sank into her awareness. She breathed, unintentionally drawing the light, floral scent of the perfume Rio spritzed all over the place, into her lungs.

Byrne wrinkled her nose.

Della's hand circled Byrne's back. 'You good?'

She nodded. 'Yeah.'

'It was bad one.' It wasn't a question.

'Bad enough, from what I can remember.'

Della tucked a stray strand of hair behind Byrne's ear. 'We have to fix that.'

Byrne sighed, wiping her mouth and grimacing at the taste of stomach acid still on her tongue. She got up. 'We tried that, and now I have more nightmares.' Water gushed as she turned the ornate, old-fashioned gold tap over the equally old-fashioned pedestal sink and cupped her hands under the flow.

As always, it surprised her that her stepmother hadn't somehow arranged for the water to be old-fashioned and gold too.

'So, we try again,' Della said.

Byrne spat water into the bowl. 'No. I don't need more. These are bad enough.'

Della was at her side, squeezing toothpaste onto Byrne's ordinary white plastic toothbrush. 'Byrne, we need to know what you know.'

'You already know what I know.' She took the proffered toothbrush and started scrubbing. The minty tang cut through the last vestiges of sour stomach acid clinging to her tastebuds, spitting and rinsing before speaking again. 'The City fell to the Horde and we lost.'

Della's hand found her shoulder, once again rubbing gentle circles as Byrne leaned back over the sink to rinse again. 'Byrne—'

She shrugged Della's hand off, dislodging the warm beginnings of magic along with it, and glared at her best friend in the mirror. 'First Nova, and now you? Stop manipulating me.'

Della stepped back, holding her hand against her chest like it had been burned. 'I'm not manipulating you, Byrne,' she said. 'You know that.'

Byrne pushed away from the sink, spun around ready to grab Della's hand and shove the azure glow of the High Priestess in her face—

Della's hands were... just hands, regular human hands. Long-fingered, the nails tipped bronze and filed into half-moons, with no trace of magic sparkling in the air around her knuckles. Byrne grabbed them, turned them over... Nothing, just amber skin, not even a hint of the High Priestess's tattoos.

Della tugged, and Byrne let her hands fall. 'Satisfied?'

'I... ' She shook her head unsure what, if anything, she was saying no to. Or if she was just trying to dislodge the mistrust from her gut. 'Sorry—'

The door rattled, Byrne's half-sister thumping the wood with her fist. 'Hey, are you finished puking yet? Some of us have places to be.'

'No!' Byrne yelled back. 'Use Dad's bathroom.'

'*You* use *Mum* and Dad's bathroom. All my stuff is—'

Della handed her the wastepaper basket and without a word Byrne swiped the collection of tubes and compacts off the little shelf above the sink.

She jerked open the door and shoved the basket into her younger sister's stomach, hard enough to make the smaller girl grunt. 'Here, make yourself pretty. God knows you need all the help you can get.'

If the look on Rio's face – a delicate combination of Japanese eyes and their father's sharp Korean cheekbones – could have been weaponised, Byrne would never have to worry about the Horde again.

'Looks who's talking, Betsy.' Rio shoved the basket back, using a strength belied by her small frame. 'I need my hairdryer, and I am *not* using Mum's shampoo. So here, take this and your fellow cow—' Rio smiled at Della, the expression enough to cut the Horde Lord to pieces. '—and go make yourself...' Her face scrunched up, like she'd smelled something bad. 'You know what, I can't think of anything nice to say.'

'Rio.' Warning sounded in Byrne's voice, and somewhere deep inside, she felt Az rise, lifting through the anger and frustration that accompanied her earliest memory of Rio. She stepped into her sister's space, trapping the basket between them, the hard plastic edge digging into her stomach. Had the gratification of seeing the younger girl's eyes widen. 'Get lost.'

Rio pushed back. 'It's *my* bathroom too, and I wasn't the one who slept in.'

Az smiled. It should have alarmed Byrne how easily the other half of her took over her face, pulled her lips back from her teeth. It didn't.

Remember me. That honey-smooth voice whispered in her ear, and realisation dawned. The speaker hadn't been talking about themselves, they'd been talking about *her*, about the Sword – about Az. *Remember* you.

Rio tried to push the basket back at Byrne, tried to use it to push her away. Byrne let her, moved back a half-step, Az riding her muscles, her eyes on the soft spot just behind Rio's ear and how it aligned with the hard doorjamb, and when her little sister went to slip past—

'No.' Della was there, pulling Byrne back and pushing Rio not just out of the way, but into the open shower cubicle, slamming the glass door shut behind her.

As Rio scowled and started pounding on the glass, Della put her back to the door. 'No, Byrne, not her; you can't hurt your sister.'

She snarled, and in that sound, there was no Byrne, there was just Az and the darkness holding the scattered bits of her soul together, hungry for flesh and blood. 'You're in my way, Mur.'

It was Della's turn to pale, for her eyes to widen. Was it fear or the shock of hearing her other name bleeding through the whites of her gaze? Whatever it was, Byrne absorbed it, felt the darkness bare its teeth – a balm to the soul.

'I know what you're doing to the girl.' The voice coming out of Byrne's mouth was hers but the words belonged to the cold-dark. 'I don't mind, really I don't. It brings me a little closer to you, to Jaya.' She slid up close to Della, belly to belly, nose to nose. 'A little more of me bleeds through the veil every time you play with her mind, but if you don't let me have my fun...' Byrne's mouth stretched and the sensation was weird, was wrong, felt like it had too many sharp, pointy teeth.

She pressed closer to Della, reaching around her for the shower door. 'You're going to wish you hadn't let me out, Mur. Going to really appreciate what the girl has been warning you about all along, and then...' The darkness leaned in close, mouth to Della's ear but its gaze... it gaze was on the little girl behind the glass, her large brown-black eyes almost popping out of her face. 'There's a price to the Wheel, Mur. You escaped it only because I took the pain for you. Deny me, and bad things will happen. Very.

Bad. Thing—'

Pain. Electrifying, sharp. Gripping her insides and spreading through her skin, turning it to fire, and her bones... Her bones were molten, were burning through her muscles, oozing out of her fingertips, her ears, her hair—

Byrne woke on the floor, cheek pressed to the tiles, heart beating loud, breath coming hard and fast through a throat that felt scorched. Her muscles shook as though she'd run a marathon, her bones ached as if she'd spent the day lifting hundred-kilo weights and queasiness gripped her stomach.

Della was at her side, holding her hair, her palm cool and comforting against the back of her neck. 'It's okay, Byrne, just breathe. The nausea will pass, it always does.'

Byrne blinked, breathed as she was told and pushed herself off the floor. For a moment, starlight swam before her eyes and she swayed.

Della was there, warm hand against her shoulder, holding her up.

'What happened?' Byrne asked, once the dizziness passed.

Della rubbed Byrne's shoulder. 'You had another nightmare,' she said.

'Another—' Byrne frowned at the wastebasket near the bathroom door, the tubes of mascara and lipstick scattered across the tiles. A nightmare? She remembered... Rio and a force that had risen from the depths of her being, cold and anger and a killing rage. 'Just a dream?'

'Just a dream,' Della said again. 'You knocked some of your sister's stuff off the sink trying to get to the toilet before you threw up. Don't you remember?'

'I— No, no I don't.' She rubbed her head. 'I must have sleep-walked or something.'

'It's okay, I was here.' Della smiled. 'Although your step-mum might be a bit freaked out, you did just kinda push past her.'

'Did I?' Confusion wrapped around Byrne's thoughts, a dark, cold film that made thinking hard, like she'd forgotten something, something more than just the dash to the bathroom. For a moment, as Della helped her to her feet, she thought she remembered Rio in the shower, fear making her eyes wide, turning her skin a ghastly shade of beige, and felt... Byrne shook it away, the afterimage of her little sister with it.

'She was pretty cool about it. Hey.' Della shook Byrne's shoulder. 'It's all right, it was just a dream. You get those all the time.'

'I don't know, Della. It feels different this time.' She put a hand on the bathroom door, pushing it back into the frame as Della turned the handle. 'I think I'm losing control.'

Darkness passed through Della's eyes, there and then gone, fast enough that Byrne wondered if she'd imagined it. 'Don't be silly.' She gave the door a tug.

Byrne stepped back, let Della push her through it.

Rio was on the other side, brows creased, perfect cupid bow lips pressed tight in an angry frown. 'Finally.' Her sister pushed past. 'It better not smell like puke in here.'

Byrne ignored her. The Sword rolled in her gut and she frantically pushed her down, down and down and down into the deepest, darkest pit of her soul. Even as she did it, she knew it wouldn't be enough, that nothing would ever be enough.

Her bedroom door shut.

She turned. The fear spilled out of her mouth. 'I'm losing control.' She held up a hand, stopping the words forming on Della's lips. 'It's not just the dreams anymore. When I train...' She trailed off, remembering the phantom sensation of Ahriman forming in her hand, the imagined demons. 'She's there, more and more. She *wants* to come out, Della, and I'm afraid that one day... One day I'm going to slip and she's going to take over and then...'

'Then want, Byrne? What's the Sword going to do?'

Blood, blood and body parts strewn across a marble floor, ichor seeping past her shields, burning her clothes, her skin. The meaty, fatty stench of flesh eaten by acid. The memory bloomed behind her eyes, clear and strong. Strong enough for her to taste the bloodlust, to *feel*, not just the sharp burning pain of wounds, but the thud of her heart, the heavy, intoxicating promise of violence. And deeper, more frightening, the knowledge that it wasn't over, that she had one more person to kill.

'She's going to kill someone.' The words tumbled off Byrne's lips. 'She *has* to kill someone, someone from before.'

'Before what, Byrne? From the first life?'

'I... ' She shook her head, the moment of clarity dissipating like smoke. 'I don't know. I just know that if she gets out, they're going to die.'

Della grabbed Byrne's hands. 'You have to give me more, Byrne.'

She shook her head. 'I don't know any more.'

Lie. The whisper rose from the depths, small and dark, redolent with blood and violence, turning her heart cold. *Lie*, it said again.

'Byrne—'

'No!' She ripped her hands free of Della's. 'No,' she said again, and wished she knew who she was talking to. The whisper or her best friend.

She turned away, snatching the yoga pants off the back of the dressing table mirror, revealing her own face. Not pointed enough to be heart-shaped, her chin too broad, cheekbones too prominent and her eyes... Dark, dark enough to obliterate light. If she looked hard enough, would she see the Sword? Would she be able to pull the warrior's secrets out, or would she just lose herself to the madness?

Maybe you would be free.

Chapter

The first rays of dawn filled the horizon beyond the wall of windows, the sky's great black dome lightened purple and orange with the rising sun. The shadows outside were grey and long, cast by the flickering carpark lights at the end of the tall poles, pierced by the harsh white car lights and the red eyes of brake lights. In contrast, the aerobics room was a beacon of light. The subtle hum of the overhead fluoros flooded the large room, pressed on the back of Byrne's eardrums in an almost perfect counterpoint to the slap and stomp of her bare feet on the parquet floor.

She spun through the kata – strike, block, grab, strike again – sweat sticking her t-shirt with its big-eyed, black, anime cat to her back, the long, braided tail of her hair whipping around her. Her legs – clad in full-length gym pants – were slashes of black lightning in the long wall of mirrors and her fists, in their black boxing wraps, were sledgehammers as she chased the dark whirl of secrets in her mind.

Remember me. The whisper had followed her through yesterday and the day before, along with the shrouded memory of Rio's scared, pale face behind the shower door; sharp, little pinpricks of cold and dark skittering up her spine.

Leap. Kick. Slide under an imaginary return strike.

Remember me.

Remember who? It wasn't like she could forget the Sword, the warrior paced the edges of her soul – a cold, blood-thirsty beast. How had she, Byrne, ever been like that? What happened in her past lives to twist the person she was now, into the Sword? Or was it that her past lives had shaped the Sword into Byrne? Or, maybe, Byrne was an elaborate hoax, an illusion to hide the devil underneath?

Would the self she knew – would Byrne – die when the mask came off? Or would she be like the Sword was now, stuck in her own body, beating her fists bloody to get free?

Punch, block, spin.

Adrenaline fuelled her muscles, fear and exertion made her heart pound, and filled the early morning shadows with monsters.

A demon charged from the corner – a squat, two-legged creature with a massive plated head and horns that could tear through a car door. She waited a beat, let the heavy *thunk* of its feet fill her, calm her heart, and when it was close enough for its rotten-egg stench to hit her nose, she moved.

A leap sideways, taking advantage of the blind spot created by those massive horns, Ahriman's heavy weight settling in her hands – hands that were bigger, stronger, knuckles calloused, backs lined with scars. Wait for the beast to draw abreast and then lunge. The tip of Ahriman's long curved blade found the weak spot at the creature's nape, slicing through the thinner armour like butter.

The demon was dead before its head rolled over the gym's parquet floor, but she didn't care. She was already spinning to meet the next one, and the next and the next.

Somewhere in the back of her brain, Byrne knew the battle wasn't real, that the demons shredded like smoke as soon as they died. That knowledge frightened her, because even though the demons were imaginary, Ahriman felt real, as real as her changed hands, as real as the cold, deadly brutality flowing through her veins. As real as the Sword taking hold of her bones, as the *pound, pound, pound* of her heart—

That wasn't her heart.

Byrne stopped, sweat stinging her eyes, breath rasping in her throat. The Sword and the demons were gone in an instant, leaving only the incessant, metallic pound.

She looked up toward the massive, glassed wall.

The sharp rattle of the old steel-framed glass only stopped when she met the steely gaze on the other side.

Ice blue eyes under dark brows and boy-band-blonde hair stared back.

Shit.

Shane.

The sparring session.

She froze, a confused mix of fear, anticipation, and something else, something deep and old and alien coursing through her nerves. How much had he seen? What had he seen? Had Ahriman actually materialised—

Another thump on the doorframe, and a furrowed brow added to Shane's stare. It was no wonder she hadn't noticed him earlier, dressed in a black hoodie and sweatpants, he was just another shadow in the pre-dawn morning, leaving his pale hair and equally pale face to float in the darkness.

He crossed his arms and pointed at the massive clock on the gym wall.

Byrne followed the direction of his finger.

Six eighteen.

'Shit.' She spun around and scrambled for the ring of keys under her sweat towel. 'Shit, shit, shit.' She was across the gym floor, pulling deadbolts and twisting the key in the lock a half-minute later. 'Shit.'

She flung the door open. 'Sorry,' she said. 'I didn't hear my alarm—'

'Whatever. I'll just come around here next time. Make it easier.' The boy had already marched across the gym floor and dropped his bag next to hers, kicking off his sneakers and ripping his hoodie over his head, leaving the dark fabric piled atop his gear.

He wasn't wearing a T-shirt underneath, that thought hit Byrne much like a sledgehammer to the face as she stared at his back. Not even a shirt or even one of those stupid, skinny-strapped muscle tees that looked like they'd tear at the slightest tug. Nope. Just pale, naked skin and black sweats that hugged his butt and thighs.

'Shit.' She was really glad he had his back to her as she checked her chin for drool.

He turned. 'What?'

Shit, had she said "shit" out loud? And shit, were her eyes actually stuck to the outline of his abs under all that smooth, porcelain skin or could she get them higher, to his nipples maybe, or hell, even his chin?

She shook her head, skirting around him for her water bottle, opting to look at the floor instead.

Byrne lifted the bottle to suddenly parched lips and reminded herself not to choke as she caught another glimpse of all those lean, wiry muscles in the mirrored wall, gleaming under the gym lights. She could only be grateful he wasn't looking at her, focused instead on winding long, black boxing wraps around his hands and between his fingers. The muscles in his chest flexed with each movement and—

He met her gaze in the mirror. 'Those moves you were doing? Looked like you might have been practicing with a bo staff?'

The question threw ice on her hormones. Shit. The questions came again. How much had he seen? Had Ahriman actually materialised?

Byrne cleared her throat. No, if he'd seen Ahriman, he'd know the weapon was no staff. 'A glaive,' she said. 'I was shadow fighting.'

He nodded. 'Right. Let's do that then – shadowbox.'

She put her bottle down and turned to face him, frowning. 'I thought you wanted a sparring partner.' He hadn't seemed the type to want to engage in imaginary fights.

He shrugged. 'You were throwing a couple of different styles together and I'd rather not get my face caved in on our first session. We'll get to the real stuff after.'

'Fine.' It was for the best anyway. If she put hands on him, she might forget he was a stuck-up prig. 'You need to warm up?'

'I jogged here. I don't like to waste time.' The rebuke in his voice, and the quick glance at the big clock, was enough to cut.

She smiled, the expression more teeth than lips. 'After you,' she said and gestured to the gym floor.

Shane Nikolov even sweated pretty. No blotchy, lobster-red cheeks, no messy flattened hair, just perfect little beads of moisture running down the hollow of his abs, sticking his hair up in spikes where he'd run fingers through it. The worst of it, though, was the faint sheen it lent his body, just enough for the overhead lights to pick out the ridge of his pecs and—

She crouched, swept his feet from under him and spun, leg still out, heel posed like a fleshy hammer over—

'Yield!' Shane thumped the floor with his palm. 'I yield,' he said again around gasps for air.

Byrne twisted, neatly retracting her foot from the air above Shane's face, and rose. Her own breath was coming fast and sweat rolled down her back and clung to the groove above her lip.

They'd moved on from shadowboxing fast enough. Almost without words, they shifted from dancing around each other, stopping their fists and feet mere hairsbreadths before they connected, to full-contact strikes. She'd never sparred like that before, never felt that kind of... intimacy. Byrne didn't know how else to describe it, but after the first ten minutes of imaginary fighting, it had been as if she'd fought with Shane for years, knew his movements as well as her own. Never had she experienced that, not even when she sparred against Sensei Joan, whose dojo she'd practically grown up in.

A small part of her, a tiny voice in the back of her head, said that was concerning, that she should be worried how easily the two of them fell into sync. But she ignored it because Az... The Sword hadn't made a peep, not one word of alarm, no bloodthirsty impulse to drive her fist through his face and stomp on his head. The relief of that was enough to make her giddy.

Byrne turned away, walking back over to the mirrors. 'I liked that last move,' she said as she bent, snatching towels and water bottles off the floor. 'You almost had—'

The rest of the sentence died when she turned to find Shane at her back. Right at her back, not even six inches of air between them. Maybe, if he'd been staring at *her* instead of the towel in her grip, she'd have taken him down – a hard punch to the gut, a knee to the face and just enough pressure on the big veins in his neck to make him pass out; a reflexive action more familiar to her than plastering her sweaty chest to his. Instead, indecision froze her to the spot, alarm racing through her veins, firing up her muscles, clenching her hands, even as it held her back.

She couldn't hit, or kiss, someone for staring at a towel.

Shane grabbed the white terrycloth from her grip.

'You drop your guard after you drop your opponent,' he said, mopping his face. He brushed past her and reached for his gear on the floor. 'I'll remember it next time.'

She hadn't even heard him get up. How had she not heard him get up? In the back of her brain, the Sword stirred.

She knew him. And was that Az, or was it the little voice of concern, the worry springing up in the back of her mind?

Of course, she knew him, she'd just spent the last half-hour beating his perfect white arse silly. And still... for the space between heartbeats, he shimmered, and the boy with his back to her was a man, and that short white-blonde hair spilled down a back clad in silk and gold—

'Same time tomorrow?'

Byrne jerked her attention back to the gym. 'What?' She shook her head, changed it to a nod mid-shake. 'I mean, yeah. Same time.'

He nodded, not even looking at her and already halfway to the door. 'See you then.'

See you then.

Anticipation shivered down her spine.

Shit.

Chapter

Wordsworth was on the blackboard in Ms Anjali's long, flowing handwriting, but Byrne struggled to see it. The blackboard was a smudge of blue-grey and the precise white chalk lines that, rumour had it, Ms Anjali practised with the same dedication Mr Mulryan demanded of his calligraphy students. Which wasn't a surprise, since the two were rumoured to be in torrid, long-term relationship, the ups and downs of which the students tracked by the pop-quizzes and long movie classes that each of the teachers sprang on them.

Whenever Ms A was on the outs with Mulryan, the poems on the board would be Plath or Poe, long and tragic or short and dark, and when they weren't... Well, they got Wordsworth.

Like now. The words on the blackboard might have been a barely comprehensible flowing mass, but they were printed well enough on the worksheets Ms A had handed out.

Up! Up! My Friend and quit your books!
Or surely you'll grow double:
Up! up! my Friend, and clear your looks;
Why all this toil and trouble?

Why all this trouble indeed. The morning sparring sessions with Shane exhilarated her as much as they wore her out. For the first time in a long time, she sparred without Az whispering in her ear. As much as she knew she should stop, as much as she knew, right in the pit of her being that this respite wouldn't last, she couldn't.

She bet Wordsworth hadn't been plagued by these decisions when he'd written his poem. Even less likely for him to be battling a ravaging Horde of interdimensional demons at the dawn of the 1800s or been haunted by nightmares and the ever-present spectre of death. Maybe Byron, with his dark poetry and troubled love life had. Or even Shelley.

Had Frankenstein been a demon, some kind of escapee slipping through a rift to make trouble in the human world? A refugee, perhaps, from their time in France?

They *had* been in France, a small village in the mountains. She remembered the way the snow had covered the ground, the lowing of the cows, the corsets and petticoats, the noble boy from the local family coming to court her on Sundays. She remembered how he died, with his chest ripped open and his heart still beating while a demon stood over him. She'd never forget what had happened after – the images haunted her nightmares the way those of Az's last battle did, perhaps more. More vivid, more... recent?

Had the French life been the last one or was that the life in Africa? It was hard to tell, all she had were flashes, little snatches of horror interspersed with the peaceful times, the ones of family and kisses stolen in the barn.

'Ms Davin.' The voice rang in the classroom. 'Ms Davin.' Again it sounded, closer this time, perhaps a little more piercing than before. 'Ms Davin.' A large white blob replaced the blurry outline of the blackboard with its Wordsworth in fancy white chalk.

A *snap*, fingers clicking in front of her face.

Byrne's eyes focussed, attention coming back from the dream-memories of grassy fields and blood-soaked stables to the bright green eyes and wide, pink cheeks of the middle-aged woman in front of her. Ms A would have made a good French aristocrat, eating cake while the poor starved.

'Ms Davin,' Ms A said again once Byrne's eyes had finished refocusing. 'Meditation practise is for your yoga classes, not English Literature.'

'Sorry—'

'Wordsworth, Ms Davin, what was he trying to convey with *The Tables Turned*, do you know?'

She did, or at least she had, she'd studied it just the other night, turned the pages of the English Lit book and pondered the—

'Ms Davin!'

Byrne shook her head, even as giggles flowed through the classroom, the only one in the school with individual desks and chairs, untouched by the modern redo that had hit the rest of the campus. Rumour had it Ms A had something to do with that.

'Umm...' she said, brain searching for the threads of last night's study.

'Yes?' Ms A's faint red brows rose, the flush in her cheeks rising with them, until she looked like a clown under the liberally applied blush. 'Is "umm" all you have for us? Or perhaps you would like to regale us with a precise and cutting commentary on Wordsworth's view about the acquisition of knowledge, dear girl? Hmm?'

Byrne's heart was beating hard, her back on fire with all the attention focused on it while she flailed for words.

Despite Wordsworth, Ms A and Mulryan must be on the outs, was the only thought going through her mind as she stared into the expectant green eyes on the other side of her little desk.

In the periphery of her vision was Fion, school blouse done up to her chin, shoulders hunched and doe eyes wide behind her thick black glasses. She'd scooted over as far as she could on her hard little chair, afraid Ms A's attention would land on her.

And it would, if Byrne didn't get her tongue unstuck quick enough, Ms A would swivel her short, fat neck and those bright green eyes would find Fion, unerringly seeking out the softest target.

Az stirred in Byrne's belly.

It would be wrong to summon Ahriman. Wrong to slam her palm into Ms A's nose and stomp on her throat just because the woman was getting in Byrne's face. She'd stared down demons, slaughtered a Horde scouting party just last week and pounded a pretty white boy into the ground only this morning. She could face down this, all she had to do was open her mouth and—

'He was talking about how nature and experience are better teachers than books.' The voice came from the back of the class; a slow, male drawl that spoke of confidence. 'He's saying that reading is good, but if you really want to learn, you need to be out in the world, applying your knowledge.'

Ms A's thin red brows un-scrunched from over her nose, and that beady green gaze lifted from Byrne's flushed face. 'Indeed, Mr Randall. A nice analysis, and tell me, how does...'

Ms A moved away, her short, heavy strides taking her to the back of the class.

Byrne breathed, concentrating on her racing heart, on the Sword rising in her soul. *Breathe in. Breathe out.*

A nudge, a pointy fingernail between her shoulder blades. 'Meditation is for yoga,' Della whispered from behind, even as a wash of calm spread from the other girl's finger, reaching for the knot in Byrne's heart.

She smiled – even though Della wouldn't see it from where her best friend sat behind her – and concentrated instead on the class and Wordsworth.

The boy at the back, the one who'd come to her rescue, knew his stuff, and more than just the LitNotes version. There was respect in Ms A's voice, and Byrne could almost imagine the delight turning the green lasers of her eyes a little bit kind. With her heart and the Sword under control, Byrne turned in her seat.

It wasn't Shane. Somehow, that was disappointing, and

disturbing that somehow, she'd expected him to be the one who came to her rescue. No, the guy at the back was familiar in that pass-him-in-the-school-corridor way, and she *felt* like she should know his name, but it refused to form in her mind.

Chestnut hair, eyebrows like slashes of darkness, wide cheekbones, pointed chin, blade of a nose, and still... That tingle of recognition, and something else...

A shift in the conversation. Ms A had finished her promenade between the rows of chair-desks and was turning around, large arse almost brushing the sides of the little tables. A girl up the back made a mad lunge for her pen as Ms A's skirt caught the edge of their workbook, but no faces were made, no snickers or snide half-whispers, as the teacher waddled her way back toward the front.

In the confusion, the boy's eyes met hers. Serious as they were dark, and that little thing in the back of her mind whispered, *Hello.*

He nodded.

Like he'd heard her.

She jerked back to face the blackboard.

'And so,' Ms A said. 'What do we take from Wordsworth's assertion that "we murder to direct"? An essay, six hundred words by the end of the week.'

The bell went, three short wails.

Byrne was out of her chair and out of the classroom before the sound finished bouncing off the walls.

The Entrance Hall was quiet, filled with the light hubbub of conversation rising from the floor below.

Eyes closed, Byrne leaned back in the corner made by window alcove and bookcase, letting the sun soak her face and warm the bones beneath. It was nice being here, a moment of peace in the endless rush and grind of Sword and school.

She could breathe, could feel just herself, the essence of the girl known as Byrne, without the rising shadow of the Sword. The sun did that, she was sure of it, sure as she was that it wouldn't last. But for now... For now, there was the warm sunlight and no one around to pester her with questions or stare at her with brooding eyes. Nothing to punch, nothing to kill, no Wordsworth, no maths, no chemistry.

For now, she could imagine what it would be like to be Byrne Davin, ordinary girl from an ordinary family, whose biggest worry was her grades and what university she was going to get into year after next. *If* she got in. Would she still go? Become the biologist her dad always wanted, or maybe a lawyer or accountant or—

Shoes on the floorboards. The sharp clack of heels. Then the heavy *plop* of a bag before someone blocked the light.

She opened her eyes.

Nova, long black hair swept over her shoulder, falling to her waist, glossy and perfect with not a single strand out of place. She stared down at Byrne.

'You're in my light,' Byrne said.

Truth, whispered the voice in her gut, and it didn't mean the sun streaming through the window.

Fuck.

Nova turned her head to the side, considering for a moment. There was something in her expression, the way she wrinkled her nose and pursed her lips that told Byrne she was arguing with herself, before she reached down and grabbed Byrne's arm.

'Get up,' Nova said. Her tug on Byrne's forearm was more jerk than anything else, half-pulling her arm from its socket.

Byrne yanked back, but Nova's grip only tightened, the sharp crescents of her nails biting into Byrne's flesh.

'Ow. Those are meant to be fingernails Nova, not fucking claws.'

The other girl only grunted and tugged again, although this

time without the nail-digging pain.

'Just get up,' Nova repeated, a certain resignation in her tone.

Still, Byrne refused. Suspicion wound up her spine at Nova's tone, and some part of her whispered for caution. 'Why?' she said.

Anger creased Nova's brow and thinned the perfect peach of her lips. 'Why the fuck do you have to be so difficult? Just do it, all right?'

Slowly, with that whisper of caution rising louder in her ears, Byrne got to her feet.

Nova tugged her over to the railing ringing the upper floor's balcony and pointed to the foyer below.

Students milled, but not many. Most of the student body was in the cafeteria, raising the roof with their insane babble, but a few senior grades and a smattering of juniors found their way to the old Entrance Hall, seeking quiet. They grouped together in little clusters, lunchboxes or travel cups in their hands, some with trays, taking advantage of the light and warmth coming through the big, mullioned windows and the benches scattered about.

'What am I—' Byrne began.

Nova nudged her shoulder and pointed again, this time towards the foyer's back, to a corner half-hidden in shadow... and a pair of long legs, crossed at the ankle. Black shoes gleamed in the sun, the laces tied in the kind of neat bow Byrne could never manage, while the rest of the body disappeared into the darkness cast by the bookcases to either side. She squinted, following the line of the legs to the boy in the shadows.

It took a moment for her eyes to adjust to the difference in light, but when they did... Chestnut hair, long pointed jaw and dark slashes for brows. The boy from English Lit, Randall something, or was it something Randall?

He appeared to be studying his shoes – maybe he was analysing his lace-tying abilities, calculating the perfect angles and tension to prevent them from coming undone. He looked the type, kind of, what with the half-frown between his eyes and the serious set to his mouth. The hair threw her though, made her rethink the perception – the messy just-got-out-of-bed-and-threw-it-into-a-pony-tail look at odds with the perfection of the crisp pleat ironed into the front of his pants.

Byrne studied him for a moment, confusion replacing some of her caution, before turning to Nova.

There was a peculiar expression on her sister-from-another-lifetime's face, a nervousness behind the stony façade. She didn't meet Byrne's gaze, instead she pointed her chin at the boy, the Empress addressing a subject. 'Who's he?' Nova asked.

'How should I know?'

'You have a class with him.'

'English Lit, and I have classes with a lot of people.' She looked again at the boy and recalled the niggle in the back of her brain. 'Is there a reason I should remember him?'

Yes, whispered the Sword.

No, no there wasn't.

Liar. I remember, and so could you, if you wanted.

She shook the thought, the temptation away and turned back to Nova. 'Why do you want to know?'

For a second, Nova didn't speak, and that nervousness rose in her eyes, even as her cheeks flushed.

Nova. With flushed cheeks.

Huh, you didn't see that every day, Byrne thought as she stood to attention. 'You like him,' she said. It was a statement, no question, not even a hint of wonder in her voice.

'So?' Nova faced Byrne, and there was a youthful belligerence in her voice. 'I'm allowed to.'

'Yeah, I...' Confusion robbed some of Byrne's enjoyment of the situation. 'Why are we here then? Why ask *me* if I know him?'

'Because....' A deep breath, Nova's chest rising and falling. 'Because I want to know if he's Tellamoth.'

Tellamoth... A vision of white hair, a man standing in a ruined bedroom, two demons dead at Az's feet.

Tellamoth. For a moment, the dream smacked Byrne in the face, loud and vivid, as if it was happening then, as if the foyer was the Imperial suite and she was standing above it, the balcony some kind of metaphysical platform between herselves – the girl Byrne and the Sword. Then it was gone, leaving just the impression of itself behind, an uneasy, queasy clench in her stomach and the name, echoing in her head.

Tellamoth.

Remember me.

The boy in the shadow, long black-clad legs with his perfectly tied shoes and messy hair.

Remember you.

'No,' she said, and heard the certainty in her voice, the conviction in her chest even as wonder made her head light. 'No, he's not.'

'You sure?'

'Yes.' Positive, right down the core of her being – right down to core of the *Sword's* being – and that scared her.

Silence, a kind of tense expectation in the air between her and Nova.

And then a breath, rushing out of Nova's mouth, taking the tension with it. Then Nova's arms were around Byrne's shoulders and her sister-from-another-lifetime was hugging her like she wanted to squeeze every ounce of joy from Byrne's body, or maybe squeeze it into her, it was hard to tell.

Nova *squeeed*, the high-pitched sound enough to shatter glass, and bounced on her toes, arms still holding Byrne tight. She released Byrne, stepped back a few steps and continued with the ballerina-esque dance.

Shock held Byrne still. Some of it from the unexpected hug, more from the sight of her normally-restrained friend/sister/rival acting like a... like a not-Nova, like one of those girls in a teen-drama and not the Empress that lurked under her skin.

Nova leapt forward for another hug, her arms like fleshy bands of steel around Byrne's shoulders. 'Thank you. Thank you!' she said and released her.

Byrne didn't move, not an inch lest she trigger another disjointed little dance. 'I didn't do anything,' she finally said.

'But you did, you totally did.' And then Nova was gone, half-skipping, half-walking to the stairs down to the foyer, her gaze on the messy-haired boy in the dark.

A thread of trepidation twisted through Byrne's gut as she watched Nova go, joy dancing like dust motes in the air around her. She was so happy. So very happy.

Nova always fell in love with Tellamoth.

That thought came out of nowhere.

But Az… Az was so sure he wasn't…

But what if he was?

Byrne's gaze cut to the boy in the shadows, and even though Az's conviction rang in her head, fear made her cold.

Fuck.

Chapter 11

A giggle.

'Daddy's a'gonna kill me if'n he finds out.'

Another giggle, and a rustling in the grass. The tall, feather-topped stalks swayed in the moonlight as they tussled.

'Then don't let him find out.' The boy's accent was strange and smooth, silk against her ears, just like his pale hair between her fingers.

He kissed her.

She kissed him back.

They rolled in the grass, the cicadas all but drowning the smack of lips and—

The pendant at her neck blazed.

All of a sudden, the cicadas weren't quite so loud, and the heavy scent of rotten eggs rolled over that of the sweet, crushed grass.

Mary Beth's blood froze.

She pulled her lips from the boy's, stiffened in his arms,

He pulled himself back. 'What?' The full moon highlighted the confusion furrowing his brow, the question in his blue, blue eyes.

The ground shivered, something hard and heavy vibrating through the dew-damp soil to make her skin crawl, even under the heavy layers of wool tunic and shifts.

She didn't stare at the boy but past him, over his shoulder and knew her eyes were wide, could feel the blood leave her face and her breath shorten at the shadows blotting out the stars. The horns. The talons. The mad, gleaming eyes.

And beside them, a slice of the dark with a smile as bright and shiny as the knife in their hand.

'Time to come home, Asenath.'

Byrne woke, heart racing, breath coming short and adrenaline riding her system. But there was no shadow, no gleam of knife, no damp earth under her back or pale-haired boy in her arms. Just the high sides of one of the school library's Chesterfield armchairs against her cheek, the dark chocolate leather with its familiar scent, comforting, the soft voices raised in a distant hubbub reassuring.

No danger. No demons. No darkness. Not in this little corner of the school library, tucked away up on the second floor, almost forgotten behind shelves full of old textbooks, the kind graced with a thick layer of dust. Just the sun streaming through the small library window, climbing over her stockinged knees, the textbook in her lap, even as it filled the little alcove with warmth.

And Fion, staring at her from the opposite chair, the low, square, study table between them, covered with laptops and books and thermos.

Fion's hair was loose, the soft white-blonde locks falling forward over her face, only half hiding her expression as she stared at Byrne over the edge of her history book. There was a small frown between her pale brows, her lower lip half caught between her teeth and those gentle green eyes…

Byrne straightened.

Fion jerked, gaze immediately cast down, hair swinging forward, a curtain cutting her off from the world.

'Fion?' Byrne's voice was soft, still clouded by the unexpected nap.

The other girl slipped a finger between her lips, chewed on the end, but didn't respond.

Byrne waited. That was the way with Fion – push and she'd hide behind a waterfall of hair and hunched shoulders, like a little mouse in its burrow. But give her space and… it was amazing what those eyes saw.

'You were dreaming,' Fion said, eyes still on her book.

'I know.'

'Was it bad?'

'I… I'm not sure.' Had it been? It had felt… important somehow, but like so many of her other dreams, the more she tried to hold to it, the faster it shredded.

'Mine are bad.' Fion's head was buried in the history book, a long string of covered wagons on the front. She drew her legs up onto the chair, knees to her chest, that book still held firmly in front of her, a shield. 'Bloody. Violent. I woke Mum and Dad up again last night, because of the screaming. Not the scared scream. The other one.'

Fion looked up, and Byrne's stomach jerked, her fingers digging into the chair's high leather sides at the red thread winding through the mossy green. And she didn't have to ask what the other scream was because it was there in the spiderweb taking over Fion's eyes.

In the depths of her soul, Az rose. *Marzanna,* she whispered.

'Della wants to take them,' Fion said, casting her gaze down again, as if that one look was all the courage she had. And maybe it was. 'But I won't let her.'

'Why?'

'Because I like them.' She hugged her knees, chewed on an end of her hair. 'I'm powerful in my dreams. Strong. I like being strong.'

Byrne opened her mouth to speak, but Fion cut her off.

'You're going to say I'm strong like this too.' Again, that quick flash of green eyes, the red of a spider crawling out of the black pupil. 'But you're lying to make me feel better, just like Della trying to take my dreams.'

Quicker than Byrne could process, Fion was off the armchair and kneeling on the old woollen rug at Byrne's feet. She captured Byrne's hands in her small, soft ones, holding them tight against her neatly buttoned blouse as surely as she held Byrne's gaze.

'But I'm not scared, Byrne, and you shouldn't be either.'

'What am I scared of?'

A look from under pale brows, Fion's head tilted to the side.

The answer hovered between them.

Az.

Byrne shook her head. 'I'm not scared.'

'Liar,' Fion whispered.

'I'm—'

'Liar,' Fion said again, harder this time, louder.

In the depths of her, Az echoed the sentiment. *Liar.*

And then, as if to prove the point, a dream fragment rose to the forefront of her mind. Tellamoth standing in room full of blood. *'Remember me.'*

Fion tugged on Byrne's hands, still trapped, bringing their faces close together. 'Don't be afraid,' she said. 'And don't let Della take more of your memories.'

'What—?'

Before Byrne could process the words, a curse came from the other side of the concealing shelves. Fion moved like lightning, curled back in her chair before Byrne could blink, head buried behind her book, hair a wheaten curtain concealing her face.

'Why'd she have to come up here?' Della's voice carried through the silence.

'The books are up here.' Suun's voice, calm and precise. 'And no people.'

'You mean, no Nova.'

'That too.'

The two of them rounded the last bookshelf, Della first, Suun following.

Where the sun streaming through the mullioned window with its thick, slightly wavy glass between old wood panes warmed Della's brown skin and picked out the golden highlights in her mahogany hair – straightened, the long fringe tucked behind her ears – it danced over Suun.

Like Nova, the sun loved Suun, but where her older sister – in this life as in all the others – emitted light, like the giant furnace at the centre of the solar system was contained within her skin, Suun... welcomed it.

Sunlight glided over her face, the high rounded cheeks, the small, square chin, and hung in the shoulder-length black tresses spilling over her shoulder. It was her eyes that stood out, dark pennies ringed in midnight, the sun's warmth seeming to gather in them as if sharing its secrets, all the things it had seen and touched on its journey from the massive star.

Or maybe that was the serene, knowing expression that sat on Suun's face. Byrne hated that look, the way Suun settled it on her, like she was peeling back layers of skin and bone. It made Byrne squirm. Made Az squirm.

Suun looked at her like that now.

Inside, Az snarled.

'You–' Della pointed a long, manicured finger in Byrne's face. 'Made me walk up stairs.'

Byrne rolled her eyes, glad for the excuse to escape Suun's stare. 'You'll survive.'

'Three flights.' Della stalked to where Byrne sat, flouncing into the single-person armchair and squirming until Byrne shifted enough to make room. 'And that last one wasn't even a staircase.'

'It had stairs and a railing.' Byrne lifted her book out of the way as Della swung her legs over her knees, careful not to watch Suun as she took the armchair beside Fion. 'It was a staircase.'

'It spiralled.'

'I thought you said spiral stairs were romantic.'

Della plucked the book from Byrne's grasp and flipped through it. 'Not these ones. Not when they lead to the attic of forgotten...' She snapped the book shut and stared at the title, nose curling. 'What are you even reading?'

'Late colonial American history.'

'Why?'

Byrne snatched the book back. 'Because I can.'

'She's not reading it,' Fion spoke, still hidden behind book and hair.

Della's eyes widened in mock salaciousness. 'Oooo.' She grabbed the book again, opening to the middle page and turning it sideways. 'But where are the pictures? Don't tell me you're reading it for the *articles*?'

Behind her shield of hair and book, Fion giggled.

Della winked at the other girl while Byrne glared at Della.

'You're a riot,' she said, taking the book back.

Della's smile was serene. 'I know, honey. That's why you love me.'

'I'd sooner love a—'

'Now, now, now.' Della laid a finger across her lips. 'Not in front of the kids.' Her gaze cut to Fion and Suun.

Byrne thumped back against the chair arm. 'Why are you here?'

Suun spoke. 'We found another portal last night.'

Byrne's attention snapped to Suun, Az's right along with her, both of them meeting the other girl's dark-penny gaze without a flinch. 'Where, and why didn't you call me?'

'It was a small one,' Fion said, voice so soft it was a wonder Byrne heard it all, as the girl sunk a little bit further behind hair and book.

So Fion had known about it, which shouldn't have been a surprise, since locating portals was one of the Executioner's powers. She cut her gaze to Della and... There. Her best friend didn't look away but there was a tightness to her lips and a wobble to her brow that said Della had been there too.

And Nova... there was no way the others would have left Nova out. So, the only one left in the dark was Byrne.

Az's claws pierced the membrane, as a growl rumbled in Byrne's chest. 'And?'

Fion trembled. Della laid a hand on Byrne's shoulder, the soothing warmth of her magic flowing from her fingers—

Byrne caught her hand, squeezed the digits tight as she peeled it away, never taking her eyes from Suun. 'Why didn't you call?' she asked again.

Suun blinked, just once, nice and slow. 'It was a small portal, sister, and we didn't need your to help close it.'

'Said who? Nova?' She would, and the others wouldn't disobey the Empress, but why? Why keep her out of—

'I told them not to call you.' It was Della who spoke. Power still radiated from her skin, ghostly azure lines hovering over her cheeks, trying to seep into Byrne's bones and make its way to the anger not-so-slowly building in her chest.

And why the anger? A small, sane part of her wondered. Why was Az sinking her claws into the space between them, and why did the cold-dark roil in her gut? Why?

The wondering didn't stop the emotions building in her chest, the cold creeping through her bones.

She squeezed her friend's hand tighter, tight enough for pain to join the guilt creasing Della's brow and drive back the comfort flowing from the High Priestess's fingers. 'Stop it,' she said, the words coming out as a hiss.

The glow died. 'You told me you're having trouble with the Sword, Byrne. I just thought you could use the break.'

Liar, Az said.

'It was a small portal,' Suun repeated. 'And the Horde didn't even have time to send a scout through before we closed it. I barely even needed to be there.'

More lies, and was that Az, or was that something else slipping off her tongue, something that stank of sulphur and tasted like burnt hair?

Byrne pushed it back. 'Why are you telling me this now then, if the portal was so *unimportant*?' She spat the last word.

'Because it was a portal,' Suun said. 'And because you should know before I go to camp.'

'You're still going?' Della said. 'I thought Nova had—'

'My sister does not run my life,' Suun cut in.

'But she cancelled—'

'She did, but someone else pulled out, and they offered me the place.' Steel had more softness than the look in Suun's eyes. 'So, you needed to know, and now you do.'

Byrne, Az, and that burnt-hair aftertaste glared back. A snarl pulled the corners of her mouth.

Suun rose; a single, fluid movement worthy of the Imperial Heir, the sunlight flowing over her shoulders, seeming to wrap around her forehead in a crown made of reflected glare. She glided out of the alcove with the same grace, only stopping long enough to cast a final look at Byrne.

'Don't fuck it up,' she said, and left.

Chapter 12

It was the early hours of the morning, the few short hours when Port Wyden slept. The traffic lights on main street flicked red then green then orange for just the dried-up leaves, fast-food wrappers and the occasional hungry ghost.

Away from the main street, the town's crumbling industrial sector, dominated by empty canneries still smelling of fish despite their vacant innards and the wind howling through their broken tin sides and shattered windows, was empty of even the ghosts. It was the memories of better times that rattled the rusty, switchback stairs leading to the flat roof, the icy light of the half-moon that cast long shadows over the cracked carpark below, reaching for the eery light of the demonic portal on the far side.

That, Byrne had taken time to notice before she'd grabbed the pendant pulsing against her chest, its sharp points digging into her palm even as she summoned its magic. Now, the last tingling shreds of its power shimmered around her legs and lowered her to the ground, the girl in the hastily pulled-on sweatpants and hoodie gone, replaced by the warrior. The Sword's dark, ghostly hands tightened on her soul even as the elaborate tarnished-silver armour tightened around her torso and the black silk battleskirt fluttered against her thighs, the longer, silver-embroidered tabard reaching for her knees.

Fion

Hard-soled boots met the rough concrete of the old factory roof, Ahriman following them with a solid *thunk*.

Fion looked back, a quick sideways glance over her shoulder. 'You won't need that,' she said. Transformed, Fion's voice lost its quiet, breathless timidity, and shivered through the night. A cutting edge stained with blood.

There was nothing timid about the Fion looking out over the abandoned lot, no hunched shoulders, no hands clasped at her middle or shoved under her armpits. Just black, armour-clad legs planted wide, blonde hair intricately braided into its skull-baring mohawk, the wind blowing the waist-long ends about like it blew the red, ground-length tabard against her legs. Fion stood with her shoulders back and arms straight at her sides, gazing out over the carpark like she was waiting for something.

Byrne wondered, as she always did, if it was right to think of Fion as "Fion" when she was like this, so different from the stoop-shouldered mouse of a girl she'd been born into, or if she should think of Fion by her other name. Except "Executioner" always stuck on her tongue and "Marzanna"… Marzanna called up memories of tangled sheets and warm lips from the depths of the Sword's shattered soul.

Byrne moved closer to the roof's edge.

Over the other side of the lot, in the space where cracked asphalt and sagging fence met the overgrown field beyond, the air shimmered. A rainbow trapped in an arch-shaped mirage. The bottom of it spat, sparks flying where it met the ground, incinerating weeds and melting tar.

As she watched, its edges grew clearer, solidifying from the bottom up, the concrete fracturing as the portal drew the raw material into itself to form a doorway.

A demon portal. A rip in the fabric between realities.

It pulled at her, a sharp hard *tug* right in her middle. Deep inside, the cold and dark *tugged* back.

She shivered, wrapped her free arm around her middle. In her other hand, the runes carved into Ahriman's haft writhed.

Remem—

'How long's it been here?' Byrne asked, the question bursting from her lips, drowning out the icy whisper.

'A day.' Fion didn't look away from the slowly growing portal. Byrne was surprised she'd even taken her eyes from it long enough to acknowledge her presence. 'I sensed it forming yesterday but didn't think it would get this big this soon.'

'And Suun?' They'd need Suun and her magic to reach through the interdimensional fabric and close it.

'On that camp.'

'Did you call her?'

'Hmmm.' There was a smile in Fion's voice, a dreamy angle to the killing edge.

Byrne turned away from the demon-spewing arch forming just three-hundred metres from their feet, and stared hard.

Fion was taller like this. Whether the transformation granted her height or it was her straightened shoulders or the savage roil of barely-leashed madness that surrounded the other girl, she loomed. And even though Byrne could look her in the eye without lifting her chin, it always felt like she had a crick in her neck when she tried to meet those frozen, green pools.

Tonight, red stained the depths of Fion's gaze, the faintest spill of it turning them brown.

Fear shivered down Byrne's spine, the Sword rising from the pit of her soul to eat it so none of that emotion made it to her face, where the Executioner could see. You did not show fear to a predator.

'Fion.' She snapped her fingers when the other girl didn't respond. 'Fion,' she said again, louder, letting the Sword echo in her voice.

The green/red eyes blinked and shifted, just for a heartbeat, from the portal to Byrne.

'Did you call Suun?' she asked again.

Gloved hands flexed, and Byrne noticed the phone held in Fion's armoured grip. The screen broke with a sharp *crack*.

'No,' Fion said.

Inside, the Sword grimaced, even as the portal's pull grew stronger. Insistent.

'Shit.' And Byrne didn't know if she was swearing at Fion or the cold churn in her stomach.

She scrambled for her own mobile, grateful that it was one of the few things that seemed to survive the transition from regular girl to immortal warrior—

Fion was lightning, one moment a sentinel at her side, the next behind, armoured fist smashing into the small of Byrne's back.

It wasn't hard, the force barely enough to push her forward a few steps, but nevertheless, the *crackkk* reverberated all the way up Byrne's spine, and she knew, without checking to see the glass tinkling to the hard concrete, that her phone was toast.

Fion stood beside her once more, arms loose at her sides, gaze still on the slowly forming portal, that tiny red thread swimming in her eyes.

Bloodlust.

Shit.

Nova's words, from all those weeks ago, rang in Byrne's ears, the way she'd broken off mid-sentence when she'd said Fion's name. The stress in her voice.

And now here was Fion – soft, mousey Fion – staring at the demon gate like a tiger beside the chicken coop. Hungry. Expectant.

Double shit.

The last thing anyone needed was the Executioner going 'zerker, more interested in spilling blood than stopping the influx of demons.

She needed to fix this.

Byrne pulled the wrecked phone from its holster. The screen was a crazed mess where the glass wasn't gone altogether, the circuits underneath exposed. It wasn't calling anyone any time soon, and the portal...

Her entire being *squirmed*.

Over the other side of the lot, the arch was almost a metre high, two columns planted in the ground, the shimmering rainbow strung between them. Dark-grey chunks of rock poured up the pillars in a river of asphalt and dirt. Another few metres and the columns would fold inwards, each side reaching for the other.

Just a few minutes since she'd climbed the death-trap of a fire escape, and the portal was already big enough to drive a ute through. Whatever was coming was going to be big. A Hustler demon perhaps? Or a Felis? Maybe even a whole fucking patrol. More than just the usual scouts.

Worse, the Sword whispered and that cold, ugly knot in her gut agreed.

Shit.

Shit. Shit. Shit.

They needed to close it and close it now, but without Suun...

Ahriman sang in her hand, the symbols caved into the black metal almost alive, pulsing in time with her heart. Deep inside, the Sword pressed a hand to the thin bubble of self that held her down, sharp black nails digging into the membrane.

There's more than one way to close a portal, the Sword said.

More than one way... The portal was already partially open, she could step through, her magic would protect her from the chaos waiting to rip her apart, and once on the other side she'd plunge Ahriman into the door master. The portal would die along with the demon that created and controlled it, wink out of existence like it had never been.

And she'd be trapped, a lone human in a Universe of demons.

Better that way, the Sword said. *Easier.*

There was something in the way the Sword whispered 'easier', a certainty that partially eased the cold, squirmy knot in her belly.

Byrne stepped forward—

A hand on her shoulder, Fion yanking her back.

Byrne spun, Ahriman sweeping the ground, the end of the long spear-like haft catching the other girl's feet and sending her tumbling. The deadly black blade pointed at Fion's throat, the air around it turning to frost as the Sword rose. 'No,' she said. 'I won't let the portal open.'

For a heartbeat, maybe even just the space between, a different face stared up at Byrne, the broad cheeks and full lips of another woman rising through Fion's delicate, pale features to glare at her.

Marzanna, the Sword whispered, and there was longing in that name, a desperate kind of need that lanced all the way through her chest, begged her to reconsider—

Byrne jerked back.

The other face was gone, the desperate need with it, and then it was just Fion, blonde mohawk spilled across the grimy rooftop, not a trace of the other woman left.

Another lightning move and Ahriman was in Fion's grip, fingers wrapped around the haft above the half-metre blade.

'Wait,' Fion said. 'We need to see this.'

Byrne jerked Ahriman, trying to dislodge Fion, but the other girl's grip was steel. 'See what? The Horde rushing through, finally gaining the beachhead they've always needed?' She pulled again, spinning as she twisted the glaive, breaking Fion's hold even as the other girl rose. Byrne kicked backwards. A shudder and a grunt, the hard point of her bootheel catching her friend in the stomach, knocking Fion to the ground.

Byrne didn't wait to see how far she'd thrown her, there was no time, she had to get to the portal.

Boots pounding the rooftop, leaping atop the ledge, a massive *push* from armoured-enhanced thighs and she was flying. Not real flight, but close enough to it, close enough to cover two-thirds of the distance between the roof and the portal. Then she was plummeting to the ground, the hard shock of impact running up her legs, knees bending, kissing asphalt, the blacktop a crazed shattered mess radiating from her boots.

She was on her feet, eyes on the portal, always on the portal, only a fraction of her attention on the shadow following her through the air. A sprint, the shimmering rainbow her only focus. The portal was clearer, stronger now that it was almost complete – the columns to either side the width of lampposts, the arch overhead a hands-width from touching. Not much time, a heartbeat. Two.

She was there, plunging into the portal, the Sword rising, singing in her chest even as the intense, skin-ripping cold peeled back her face and chaos ate at her arms, her—

A hand around her bicep, hard, steel-gloved fingers *yanking* her back. Spinning, the moon above, the cracked, weed-choked parking lot, the old graffiti-covered factory. Fion between her and the portal.

The Sword in her bones, in her muscles, twisting her face. Ahriman slashing through the night, the blade tailing frost.

Two crescent moons gleaming under the stars as Fion's twin curved swords appeared in her hands, and those green eyes bled to brown.

The clash of weapons. Ahriman caught in the shielding V formed by the Executioner's blades.

Executioner and Sword snarling in the darkness.

'Wait,' said the Executioner. 'We need to see.'

'No,' said the Sword. 'We don't.'

The one buried in the other, the girl known as Byrne, pushed against the vise holding her voice, against the hard, meaty fingers squeezing her soul. But rage swamped her senses and bloodlust was every breath she took. She couldn't move, couldn't *think*.

The Sword bore down, the black sunmetal of Ahriman's blade screeched against the silver crescents of the other's swords.

The Executioner's arms strained.

The Sword grinned.

'Wait,' the Executioner said again, and there was a soft, desperate plea in her voice. 'Byrne, please, this one's different. I can feel it.'

The Sword could feel it too, clawed hands playing with her vertebrae, digging into her back, pulling out her kidneys. Pain like she'd only known once before, melting her skin. This one *was* different. This one needed to be stopped, and now, before *he* came.

In the Sword's soul, a depthless dark yawned wide and within it... The girl known as Byrne pulled back, thrashed against the grip holding her down, trapping her in own flesh. She beat against the Sword, hands and voice and every fibre of her being screaming at the other to stop. To—

In the darkness, power rippled, gathered in the Sword's hands, and for just a second, a terrifying moment between heartbeats, Ahriman glowed and a void consumed the ground at her feet.

The Executioner paled. Her swords trembled.

The Sword struck. Ahriman breaking through the crescent swords, the blade not slicing but twisting. The Sword's skirts flared as she spun, the thick black metal of the glaive's opposite end striking the other woman's temple.

The Executioner crumbled, unconscious, to the ground.

The Sword kept spinning, mind already on the portal, on what she had to do on the other side, the few seconds she'd have before the Horde ripped her apart—

A blazing sun in her path, heat and power and a girl with night-dark hair and a golden circlet on her head, a sunburst between her brows.

Nova.

The Sword snarled, the darkness in her soul rising, piercing the rays of power, the—

Another burst of light, this one softer, a shiver of moonlight, lost in Nova's glory. It was too late to turn, too late for the Sword to dodge the hands gripping her shoulders or the magic rushing through her body, beating back the darkness and commanding her to sleep. Her knees collapsed, Ahriman falling from nerveless fingers – the glaive hitting the concrete, obliterating it – and she went with it, Della at her back, guiding her down.

'Sleep, Asenath,' Della said, voice soft as the magic coursing through her soul. 'We don't need you yet. Go to sleep. We'll call you when it's time.'

'The time is now,' she wanted to say, but weariness weighed her tongue and darkened her vision. And no matter how hard she fought, the Sword couldn't stop Della's magic from claiming her.

She slept, and the girl known as Byrne slept with her.

Chapter 13

The glaive burned, not with heat or light, but with darkness. The runes carved into the black metal writhed with shadows that not even Nova's halo could dispel. Instead, they grew richer, the shapes reaching, eating what little remained of the concrete and sinking through to the rubble beyond.

The girls watched it, silent heartbeats passing as the ground continued to crack as if the glaive were an asteroid impacting the Earth in slow motion. Or maybe it was the darkness spreading its fingers. One crack reached past the hem of Nova's long, white-gold skirts reaching for her boots. The dark within the crack seemed to bathe in the light emanating from her skin, and instinct had her stepping out of its path.

Hastily, Nova dispelled her halo, willing it back into her body, and... The crack continued past her, the shadows continuing towards the portal.

'Why didn't Ahriman dematerialise?' Della asked, and Nova wondered if it was actually a question or if her friend merely wondered out loud.

Nonetheless, she answered, and when she did, none of the gut-crunching fear in her belly made it to her voice. 'I don't know.' She looked up, caught Della's gaze and reached deep inside herself for the Empress, infusing her words with power. 'But we don't ask Byrne and you will take the memories of what happened tonight to make sure.'

Duty and compassion crashed on Della's face, furrowing her brow and pulling at her mouth. 'I can't keep wiping her memory, Nova.'

The Empress rose and Nova let her, welcomed the certainty that came with her other self, burning all the fears, all the doubt as the other took over her mouth. 'You will do it,' she said and though the voice was hers, was calm and soft, it was threaded with the iron ring of command.

Across from her, still crouched beside Byrne, Della's dark face paled. 'We can't keep doing this to her,' Della said again. 'It's making the Sword stronger, and Byrne needs to know she's not going crazy.'

'We can and *you* will,' said Nova, the Empress still riding her tongue. 'Byrne will know when she needs to, when we can control the Sword.'

'Nova—'

'No.' Nova let the other all the way out, felt the Empress turn her eyes to suns and rise through her skin, making the pale gold gleam like it was the real thing. 'Do it.'

She didn't wait for Della to comply, there was no need, the certainty of it rested in her bones, and the portal at her back was shifting. She couldn't sense the portals like Fion, couldn't feel the fabric of reality parting like a never-ending itch down her spine, but the demons... Nova twisted, Avestan appearing in her hands, the sword an eye-searing blaze of fire as she slashed it across the shimmering veil.

The horned head rolled across the ground, ink-black blood spewing over the rubble, spitting as it made contact with earth.

Nova didn't stop, Avestan danced in her hands, the blazing edge singing in the air as her long battleskirts flared around her gold, nano-armoured legs. Demonic blood flew, the few drops that sizzled through the thin golden film of her personal shield, splashing against the elaborately worked amour wrapped around her shoulders and torso.

More body parts fell, more black blood soaked the parking lot and soon she had enough corpses to choke the portal. Two minutes, ten, an hour, how long she slashed and parried, Nova did not know – she did not keep track of time, did not count the limbs or heads or weapons scattered about her feet. There was only the portal, the Horde coming through, her friends and her sister at her back, and the world beyond them, all depending on her, *counting* on her to do the right thing. To win.

Slash, parry, stab. The fight was a meditation, a perfect moment when the barriers between Empress and Nova fell, and they remembered. The golden light, the man on the throne, the orb in his hand the key to ending the war, and the shadow moving between them, coming to stop them.

The darkness threatened everything Nova and the Empress held dear.

A final slash, another corpse to add to the knee-high wall of flesh and bone blocking the portal.

The shimmering arch died. The rainbow mirage flickered – once, twice, a third time – guttering out of existence like a candle. The arch itself remained a moment more, the shards of broken asphalt caught in a delicate balancing act, unsure if they wanted to lean left or right before they tumbled to the ground in a shower of dust.

When it was gone, only the corpses remained, sliced clean through where they'd bisected the portal, leaving an acrid-smelling pile of arms and torsos. The sun would take care of the unearthly beasts, burning away horns and snouts and claws, flesh both furred and scaled. In the meantime...

Byrne was stirring, and her sister's glaive... Relief sunk through Nova's chest as the weapon, with its curved black blade and long, spear-like haft, faded. It's edges blurring first, the shadows carved into the metal drawing still before it faded from sight altogether.

Nova let go of Avestan, the blazing sword winking out of existence the moment it left her grip. The Empress went with it, the other's fiery presence fading to a distant warmth, taking Nova's certainty with her.

'Della,' Nova said, and was surprised at the weariness in her voice, the way it shook. 'Byrne's waking.'

Della was kneeling beside Fion, glowing hands held over the bump on the other girl's head. 'Let her. I've done what you asked.'

Guilt stabbed at Nova's heart, but she pushed it away. She had to do this or her friends would die, and this time they wouldn't come back.

He stood in the shadows, peering through the circle he'd rubbed clean in the factory's old window, to the tableau across the parking lot.

The Empress was a beacon of light, radiant even without her halo. Majestic. Commanding.

Beautiful.

But the monster at her feet... Darkness pulsed around the Sword, the girl-woman once known as Asenath. It crept across the cracked ground, reaching for the Empress, licking at her boots. Corrupting. Evil.

His hands clenched; the desire to smash through the window built in his core. Damnit. He'd been so close, made sure to time the portal opening just right so the magic-using Heir wasn't there to close it, leaving just one option, and Asenath had leapt off the roof and pelted across the lot like her tail was on fire, heroic to the end.

If the mohawked girl hadn't stopped her, the bitch would be on the other side of the portal by now – food for the Horde. Problem taken care of. The hardest part of his mission accomplished.

But now...

'*Kel.*' The ancient profanity exploded from his lips at the same time his fist pounded the wall. Cracks radiated through the old brick, mortar and plaster raining down on him from above, even as the building itself seemed to groan.

Now he'd have to start again, plant another portal seed and wait. Next time though... He glared at the dark-skinned girl crouching over the blonde one. Next time he'd make sure no one was there to interfere.

He waved his hand and disappeared in a rainbow shimmer, never seeing the figure hidden in deeper shadows, a stray snatch of moonlight catching white hair.

Shane

Chapter 14

There was something not right with her head.

Early dawn moved across the gym floor, sweat stuck her t-shirt to her back, strands of hair to her cheeks. Images, like fractured bits of a dream, kept popping in front of her eyes. Fion on a rooftop. A rainbow portal.

Distractions.

She didn't have time for distractions.

Shane threw her to the floor.

The impact reverberated through her bones. A dull, blunt pain bloomed in her shoulder even as she rolled and—

Thwack. A bare foot where her head would have been, all bony toes, tendons and snaking veins standing out against pale, porcelain skin.

Byrne braced a hand against the parquet floor, tensed her stomach and rolled the other way. Or tried to.

Thwack. Another foot, another black-clad leg boxing her in, knee bent, balance not quite right...

She struck, elbow behind the knee, pushed up even as he fell forwards and sideways, cursing as he went down. And again, she was rolling away from Shane, trying to get to her feet. Byrne could have rolled towards him, grabbed his arms, pinned him to the floor and finished the match. She'd tried it once, had her forearm across his throat, a perfect chokehold, just a little pressure and he wouldn't have been able to breathe. Or so she thought.

The guy was slippery. Too slippery. She still couldn't figure out how he'd done it. Somehow, he'd weaselled out of the hold and before she knew it, *she* was pinned, arms and legs immobile, staring up into that perfect face, chiselled cheekbones and boy-band looks sheened with exertion, the smell of sweat and *Shane* curling around her nose.

Byrne pushed the memory away as she rolled to her feet. That had been a week ago and it was still stuck in her head.

The brief glimpse she caught of herself in the big mirrors showed her cheeks not delicately flushed with exertion, but blotched red. And there was Shane, on his feet too. *His* pretty white skin had the delicate flush, *his* hair didn't look like a demented rat had made it its home, and *fuck it*, would it kill the guy to wear a shirt?

Byrne circled left, Shane mirroring her movement, neither of them making a sound on the gym's glossy wood floor. Distantly, cars passed on the street, the rumble of morning traffic winding through the warble of the magpies roosting in the old gums dotting the carpark, but inside... Just their breathing and the hard thump of her pulse. Exertion, she told herself, just exertion. A solid hour of fighting imaginary opponents was one thing, the same time spent fighting a real-life partner was something else. Totally something else. Nothing to do with the tension in the pit of her stomach, with staring into her opponent's glacial blue eyes and watching the play of muscles across his chest. Nothing at all, absolutely noth—

He darted toward her, shoulders moving like he was going to strike, but his chest... His abdomen tightened, and so Byrne was ready, leaping instead of bracing as Shane dropped to the floor, leg sweeping the air where her legs used to be.

She came down, angled just a little to the left and— A hard

THWACK as her heel met the floor, inches from Shane's torso, cutting off his escape. And he was already turning the other way, her hands on the back of his head helping to guide him right into her knee.

They froze. Her knee a millimetre from his nose, his hand braced on her inner thigh.

He met her eyes. 'I ye—'

A loud wolf-whistle interrupted.

Adrenalin spiked, Byrne's hands turned to fists, both her feet braced on the cold parquet floor, some part of her noting Shane jumping to his feet and doing the same before her eyes locked on the figure sitting just inside the open door.

The morning sun brought out the gold in Della's cheeks, a delicate ripple of colour like magic under her skin, while the pleated school skirt highlighted the curve of her waist, and the shirt her chest. She was sitting on a school bag and leaning against the big windows, a throwaway coffee cup in one hand. From the smile stretching her lips and the knowing glint in her eye, she'd been there awhile.

Della put her takeaway coffee cup down and clapped. 'Nice show, guys.'

Byrne scowled, the tension leaving her body even as a new flush, one not brought about by exertion, heated her cheeks. 'Della, what are you doing here?'

Beside her, it took Shane another few seconds to relax his own fighting stance. One moment tense, the next... 'A friend of yours?'

Della was on her feet, a second black takeaway cup in her hand. 'Her *best* friend,' Della said as she approached, handing the second cup to Byrne. 'Coming to walk her to school, but maybe—'

'Right,' Shane said, the word short and almost... not annoyed, something else, a sound that hit the back of Byrne's ears like a dagger and had her looking up, catching his gaze.

It lasted a second, less maybe, but in that moment, she saw not the annoyance echoed in his voice but... Pain? Anger? The emotions turning the rich turquoise of his eyes dark. And then he was turning away, leaving her to stare at the hard, lean muscles of his back as he stalked to the pile of clothing and sweat towels against the wall.

He picked up his shirt, pulled it on, grabbing the rest of his gear before he turned. 'I'm going,' he said, gaze on Byrne, ignoring Della. 'I'll see you tomorrow.' He left, disappearing out the side door, shoulders stiff.

Byrne watched him go, puzzled by the anger and pain in his eyes, the tension in his shoulders. Was he angry that Della had interrupted the match? She cast a glance at the big old clock above the mirrors. The hands pointed to fifty minutes past six. They'd have stopped soon enough anyway.

She turned her attention to Della.

One arm crossed over her ribs, the other lifting her coffee, Della raised a single dark brow. 'Your tea's getting cold,' she said.

Remembering the cup in her hand, she sipped. Made a face as the bitter taste of over-steeped Earl Grey hit her tongue. 'It's already cold.'

'That's what you get when you don't tell your best friend you're spending the morning wrestling with a sweaty, half-naked guy.' Della took another sip of her coffee.

Byrne made a face. Della's coffee had to be as cold as her tea. 'How are you even drinking that?'

'It's called sugar,' Della said. 'So, when did you start wrestling with Mr Tall, Pale and Pretty?'

Byrne turned away, heading for her gym bag and the water bottle stuck in its pockets. 'We were sparring, and a while.'

'A while? So, like, every now and then a while? Or, every day a while? I mean, he *did* say "same time tomorrow" so I'm assuming it's more than once a week, right?'

'Della.' Frustration and embarrassment combined to make her voice high, and her movements rough as she jerked the bag open.

'Just... we're sparring, okay? Nothing more. Leave it alone.'

Byrne winced, realising her mistake even as the last words left her mouth. Never tell Della to leave something alone.

And there her best friend was, crouched at her side, her deep bronze gaze glittering like a wolf on the hunt. 'You like him,' she said, glee in her voice.

'Della...'

'What's not to like? I mean, he could do with a tan but...' Della turned to the still-open door like she was watching Shane leave all over again. 'Mmm. Yum.'

Byrne shoved her sweat towel in the bag and yanked it closed. She got to her feet. In for a penny, in for a pound. 'Just leave it, Della,' she said, and headed for the showers.

For a glorious half-minute, Byrne thought Della wasn't following and then...

'You're allowed to like him, Byrne.' Della was in front of her, holding open the off-white door to the women's bathroom, crossing the distance between them in the strange way she had as High Priestess – an ability Byrne could never decide was true teleportation or merely illusion.

Humidity hit Byrne in the face, adding a fresh layer to the sweat clinging to her brow, the strong smell of citrus cleaners almost, but not quite, covering the unique gym-room scent.

Byrne paused before stepping over the bathroom's threshold, yanking flip-flops from her bag and letting them fall to the gym's blue-grey rubberised floor – a soft *plop plop* – before shoving her bare feet in. The bathrooms were cleaned at night, but she needed tinea like she needed the Horde storming the showers.

For once, the bathroom was empty, all of the gym-going office workers already bundled back in their cars, joining the exhausted throng on its way to another day of toil. They left behind a damp, fog-shrouded sauna in place of the cold bathroom, it's row of plastic-curtained showers on one side and toilet cubicles on the other, with just a wooden bench between.

Byrne dumped her bag on the bench, pulling out a towel and toiletries.

Della snagged her sweat towel, setting it on the damp bench before sitting. Her hair was straight today, falling half-way down her back in a dark brown river, the overhead fluoros picking out red and gold highlights.

'Your hair's going to frizz,' Byrne said.

Her best friend shrugged. 'I'll survive.'

Byrne pulled aside the curtain covering the cubicle.

'You used to have fun,' Della said, the words a lasso, holding Byrne tight, leaving her paused with the curtain in her hand, her back to the bench. 'You used to laugh more and sneak out on dates.'

With a jerk that popped a few curtain rings, Byrne unstuck herself and dragged the thick white plastic closed. She hung her towel on a hook, her toiletries on the little ledge behind the shower head. She twisted the shower knobs. 'I have fun,' she half-yelled over the spray of water on the tiny white square tiles.

'No,' and somehow Della's voice was next to her ear even though Byrne could see her sitting on the bench, a shadow against the curtain. 'You beat things up, and you hide in alcoves, and you worry.'

'It's my job,' she whispered into the water. 'It's who I am.'

'You don't have to be the Sword all the time.'

'But I am,' Byrne said, still whispering. She held her fist to her chest. 'She's right here.'

Inside, the Sword dug fingers into the thin web that kept her apart from Byrne.

She shoved her head under the spray, wishing the pound of it would pummel the Sword back under, take over from the constant churning in her gut. It wouldn't, it never did, but maybe this time... She grabbed the little shampoo bottle from the ledge.

As she lathered and scrubbed, piling hair atop her head to scrub some more, Della spoke, voice still right next to her ear even though Byrne was alone in the cubicle.

'The Priestess is with me too,' Della said. 'She speaks to me, all the time.'

Byrne stopped scrubbing. Turned to see Della's shadow through the curtain. 'You never said.'

'I'm saying it now.'

'How do you... how do you keep her down? How do you ignore her?'

'I don't. She's a part of me. An older, stranger part, but still... me.' A pause, and there was a hitch in it, a tension that had Byrne wishing could see Della's face.

The water pounded on Byrne's back, suds streaming down her shoulders, hair slipping from the bun atop her head.

Della's silence tightened the air.

Byrne spoke. 'What, Della?'

Another moment of silence and Byrne didn't need to see Della's face anymore, she could picture the way her friend's lips clamped together, the frown between her brows as fought with herself. About what?

Inside, the Sword rolled against her restraints. *About us.*

'The Sword is a part of you too,' Della said, the words a rush. 'You *are* the Sword, are Asenath, it's just...' Della was on her feet, hand pressed to the plastic separating them. 'You need to *remember*.'

Remember.

Remember me.

Tellamoth.

'No.' Byrne shook her head, closed her eyes and stuck it back under the water. Shampoo washed down the drain.

Yes. The Sword rolled. *You can.*

Fear churned her stomach, gave her fingers extra strength as she rinsed out the last suds, grabbed the conditioner and started the whole process again. But that meant she had to step out from under the spray, couldn't drown Della's words under the rush of hot water.

'Byrne... I can help you. We can do it together.'

She ignored Della, squirted pearlescent pink goop into her hand and slapped it on her head.

'Byrne... Do you remember what happened on the weekend?'

'I studied. Maths and chemistry. And I binged that TV show.' She twisted her pink-gooped hair over her shoulder and reached for the soap.

'What was the show called?'

'I... ' Byrne shook her head, the name of the thing eluded her, which was strange, because she was usually really good at remembering names. 'I don't know.'

'What was it about?'

'Something about...' About what? Demons and shimmering portals, a smashed phone but no that couldn't be right... She rinsed the soap off her body. 'It wasn't that memorable. I think I fell asleep half-way through. Why are you asking?'

Again, that silence on the other side of the curtain.

Byrne rinsed the conditioner from her hair, the steam turning the air white and thick. Or maybe that was the trepidation running up her spine, its sharp fingers leaving ice in its wake despite the hot water pounding her head.

She shut the water off, but even as she reached for the towel and wrapped it around her body, her attention was on shadow behind the curtain.

'Della?'

No sound save the *plop plop plop* of the leaky shower head.

Trepidation turned to fear, its fingers now claws ripping into her gut, bringing with it images of demons and blood-soaked floors. Her heart pounded, the Sword rising within as she jerked aside the curtain—

And there was Della, her brown-black hair starting to frizz in the steam-laden air, wide generous lips pressed tight, indecision and something else, something like guilt creasing her brow. But no demons. No portals. No anybody. Just them. Della on the bench, hands in her lap; Byrne, the shower curtain half-ripped off the rod, the long black fall of her hair soaking her towel; and the Sword, laughing in Byrne's soul.

Relief took the stuffing out of Byrne's legs, and—

'It wasn't a TV show,' Della said.

'What?'

'On Saturday night, you didn't fall asleep watching a show.' Della took a deep breath, the indecision clearing from her brow even as that other emotion, the guilt, hardened into determination. 'You were trying to close a demon portal.'

It was Byrne's turn for silence, confusion and a disturbing sense of déjà vu holding her tongue hostage. The bathroom cooled, the wet hair clinging to her back becoming icy, just like the feeling in her gut.

Della looked so serious, so *convinced*, but it wasn't possible, she'd... 'I'd remember that,' Byrne said. She nodded, even as she plucked a spare towel from her gym bag. Inside, the Sword was silent. 'I'd totally remember a demon portal, if only because Suun calling down the stars to close it is kinda hard to forget.'

Except Suun hadn't been there.

Byrne froze as that thought sprang, not from the Sword, but the shadows at the back of her head.

'Suun wasn't there, Byrne.' Della echoed the darkness. 'And yes, usually you'd remember that, except...' She looked away, and there it was again, the guilt, pulling at the corners of her mouth, filling her eyes with moisture. 'I took your memories, Byrne.'

Chapter 15

She stood there, the steam from the shower wrapped around her ankles, hair a straight waterfall of black down to the small of her back, the heavy strands plastered to her skin. The crescent-moon pendant resting against her breastbone was the only spot of warmth as water trickled down her spine, quickly turning to ice, or maybe that was Della's words tripping over her vertebrae.

The gym bathroom had never seemed this... this *cold*. Not even in winter, when frost traced patterns on the windows and the ground crunched underfoot, and definitely not now, with summer still lengthening the days. She'd never really noticed how it echoed either, how empty it seemed this early in the morning. Della's confession bounced off the white ceiling, the floor with its small square tiles, even the plastic curtains separating the eight shower cubicles from the rest of the room, the basins with the long room-width mirror on the other side.

Della remained silent, her big, deep-brown gaze not quite meeting Byrne's almost-black one, her straightened locks starting to frizz in the steam. Her carefully ironed white shirt was unbuttoned enough to see a hint of cleavage and the deep blue tear-drop shaped pendant, with its delicate gold filagree in the shape of a tree, nestled there. Not enough to get in her in trouble with the school matron, but enough to make her stand out. That was Della, right down to the plain gold rings on each of her fingers.

Those thoughts, those observations went through Byrne's head, even as '*I took your memories'* echoed in the steam. It was shock, some part of her knew that; shock that froze her vocal cords and gummed up her brain, even as her hands tightened on the soft white towel wrapped around her from breasts to knees. *No.*

Deep within, the Sword pressed her hand to the thin membrane holding her down and whispered, *Yes.*

No.

Yes.

No.

Yes!

The chill bit at Byrne's ankles while a rivulet of water traced the broad lines of her face from brow, over the rounded shape of her cheek to gather at the point of her chin. She wiped it away. Shook her head. 'No,' she said aloud. 'You wouldn't. You *didn't*.'

It was Della's turn to shake her head, as small as the movement was. She stood from the bench, arms crossed over her chest, and her gaze skittered away from Byrne's, the lush line of her mouth flattening, her dark brown skin losing a little of its natural flush. 'I did,' she said.

'No,' Byrne repeated, emphatically this time, her voice firm. She reached past Della, snatching the other towel from her gym bag, sweeping the wet hair off her back and bending over to wrap it in the faded blue terry cloth. 'You're my best friend, and you wouldn't do that to me.'

'I would.' Della paused. Took a deep breath and pulled her shoulders back. 'I would if Nova commanded it of me.'

Just a second, it took just a second for the world to shift, for pain to split her heart in two and betrayal to turn her insides cold, for tears to gather in her eyes. Just a second, and in that second, bent over with her hands twisting the towel around her wet hair, the membrane holding back the Sword cracked.

The pain ripping her heart lessened.

Byrne stood, wrapped her towel-encased hair into a turban atop her head. She stared Della straight in the eye.

The other girl's gaze wavered, eyes skidding to the side.

'Why?' Byrne asked.

The question rang, bouncing off tiles and mirrors, only to be swallowed by the stream.

Another deep breath from Della, still not meeting her gaze. 'I—' she began.

The pale, iridescent moon resting against Byrne's breastbone vibrated.

Della's did the same.

Together the girls covered them with their hands, and when Della met Byrne's gaze, confusion and alarm were chasing away the guilt in her eyes.

'Why are they vibrating? It's daylight,' Byrne said. 'Demons don't come out in daylight.'

Della's jaw tightened, even as her fingers wrapped around her pendant, and her gaze ran around the bathroom. 'There're no windows in here,' she said. Her eyes came back to Byrne's. 'No daylight.'

Every ounce of blood in Byrne's body froze. 'Fuck.'

The last, white swirls of steam gained a new menace.

Slowly, as if any movement might trigger a rush of armoured claws, she reached for her underwear.

'We should change,' Della said, moving just as slow as Byrne, turning so she faced back towards the door leading into the gym. When she said change, Della wasn't referring to their shoes, or lack of in Byrne's case. She meant the other kind of change, from regular schoolgirls to demon-hunting warriors.

'And what if it's not demons the pendants are reacting to?' Undies on, Byrne reached for her bra, scanning every shadow, alert for the slightest movement. 'Last thing we need is for someone to get a good look at us.'

'What else could it be?'

'My boss comes in early. It could be Ray.' Even as she said it, the clenching of Byrne's gut spoke otherwise.

'Your boss isn't a demon.' The air next to Della's hand shimmered as the High Priestess's staff began to form. 'A human wouldn't trigger the pendants.'

A laugh bounced off the tiles, coming from somewhere near the door.

Every muscle in Byrne's body went rigid. She knew that laugh, the *Sword* knew that laugh, the way it rose out the villain's chest, how it shone in his eyes, how it always came just before the final blow. The way he could project it, make it come from one direction when he was right behind you.

Byrne spun, towel falling away but bra and undies on, some armour at least, no matter how flimsy, against the man at their back. Or she thought it was a man, the tall, lithe form was hazy, light rippling around him obscuring all but the barest hint of face and physique. For a second, as the lights popped and shifted, she wondered if she was hallucinating, if the hundred different pale, gem-like colours flashing before her eyes weren't some figment of an overstretched or even drugged mind. Maybe she was still dreaming, or Della had taken her memories again. Or maybe the Sword was finally taking hold and she, Byrne, was breaking.

Maybe.

No. The Sword speared cold, hard fingers through the membrane and laid them on Byrne's shoulder. *He's an illusion master.*

Like Nova, able to make people see whatever she wished, manipulating them.

Yes, and no. The Sword's certainty spread through Byrne, stiffening her spine, clearing her head, but doing nothing against the lights obscuring the man. *Not as powerful, but stronger too.*

What did that even mean?

The Sword was silent, save for one last whisper. *Tellamoth.*

'Tellamoth,' Byrne echoed.

He laughed and the sound bit her ears, reaching deep inside and stirred something, a queasy, uneasy emotion in the very pit of her being. Guilt. But why?

Behind Byrne, Della stiffened and spun about, one second a schoolgirl the next a statuesque beauty, hair a riot of glossy mahogany curls, the long skirts of her white robes flaring about armour-clad legs, pendant still glowing a brilliant blue at her throat. Della was going to be pissed after this, all that work put into straightening her hair blown with a single transformation.

The silver-capped end of the High Priestess's staff cracked the tiles. Blue lightning played around the elaborately carved pearlescent haft, wrapping around Della's tattooed hands and arms before spitting from the stone held in the thick ribbon-like swirl of silver at its top – the same blue as the pendant around her neck. Magic streamed from the stone, a brilliant bolt of power that smashed into the rainbow obscuring the form that was Tellamoth.

There was a curse, a deep grunt of pain from Tellamoth. Della's magic made him stagger before the illusion split – still concealing his face – and a glimmering bubble of power took its place. A shield against the High Priestess's attack.

Della snarled, red lips pulling back over white teeth, the muscles in her upper arms bunching as she leaned into her staff. The magic streaming from the weapon brightened, growing stronger.

Byrne watched, not moving, not grabbing her own pendant and summoning the brilliant rush of her other self like she ought. She was frozen, that queasy sensation rooting her flip flops to the tiles, holding her hands hostage at her sides. Something was wrong, something was very, *very* wrong.

Was it even really Tellamoth standing before them? Fuck, if he was here, in the bathroom, how were she and Della not dead already? Why reveal himself? Why here, why now? Why not stay in the shadows, a name without a face? Surely, if he could sneak up on them like this, he could sneak up on Nova and stick a knife in her back.

The questions ran hard and fast through Byrne's mind, even as the Sword ran thick, sharp nails along Byrne's psyche, and the upside-down crescent-moon pendant at her throat burned. Eager to change, to shuck bra and undies and uncertainty for armour and glaive and the Sword's frenzied rush.

'Change,' Della said, her voice deeper, echoing with the power running under her skin and the strain of fighting Tellamoth. And although her gaze never left Tellamoth's light-obscured form, the words were for Byrne. 'Now, I can't keep him busy forever.' What she didn't say was 'Before he figures out your real identity.' But if he was here, in the gym's bathroom, he already knew.

Some instinct, some whisper, made her hesitate. If this was Tellamoth, transforming in front of him would be bad, she knew it deep in her soul, in a place beyond the darkness, beyond the Sword, where the queasiness rolled.

Breath on the back of her neck.

Illusion master, the Sword whispered. *Distraction is his weapon.*

Byrne turned.

Tellamoth smiled at her, dark eyes, full lips and the knife rushing at her middle all she could see through the shattered mirror of his illusion.

She was already stepping back, hands coming up to block the strike, stomach tightening, but not fast enough. Nowhere near fast enough, and no matter how rigid she made her abs, no matter how the muscles stood out against her skin, they weren't going to stop the gleaming edge of the knife from sinking into her gut.

This was going to hur—

A shadow crashed into Tellamoth, a body dressed in black with pale hair tackling him from the side. The knife grazed

Byrne's stomach, and then Tellamoth and... Was that *Shane* rolling about in the still-wet shower cubicle, pounding his fist into the kaleidoscope that was Tellamoth's face? His normally stony expression was a snarl, and damp stuck his black hoodie to his back while his short, white-blonde hair was a wild explosion atop his head.

He punched again, Tellamoth blocking the blow, the villain's other hand coming back up, knife gleaming in the overhead fluoros.

Byrne was there, kicking the knife from his grip, foot raised to stomp—

Her heel met tile, the white ceramic breaking with a sharp *crack*, instead of the fragile cartilage of nose and face. Tellamoth was gone, vanished as readily as he'd come.

She spun about, expecting another attack from behind— Only to see Della, magic still cracking around her arms, hands still locked tight around her staff. Their gazes met, just for a second, before they continued scanning the bathroom, both of them alert for the slightest hint of movement, the first tell-tale twist of gem-like lights.

Seconds passed. Nothing, save the blood hammering in her ears, the growing chill sinking into her skin at odds with the warm breath against her stomach.

Byrne looked down.

Shane still knelt on the tile, hands held at his sides like he wasn't quite sure what to do with them, or maybe he was just trying to figure out where his opponent had gone. Whatever he was wondering, confusion wrinkled his brow, while suspicion drew his eyes tight as they met hers.

They stared at each other a second, neither of them blinking.

For a heartbeat, as her hair spilled forwards in a dark curtain, and she fell into the glacial blue of that gaze, the uneasy, queasy feeling in her soul, beyond the darkness, beyond even the Sword, settled and another emotion bloomed in its wake. The warmth of it slipped through her veins and bought a flush to her skin. And was that an answering spark in Shane's eyes, did he lift his head towards her even as she leaned down?

Silver cracked on tile, the smell of burnt ozone filling the air.

Byrne jerked backwards, cursing at the sudden bloom of pain as she slammed her shoulder into a towel hook screwed into the cubicle wall. Ignoring the pain, she faced outwards, to the bathroom proper, aware of Shane leaping to his feet and doing the same.

Della stood there, stance wide, the end of her staff planted firmly on the floor. Even though the fight was over, magic still crackled around her arms, the High Priestess's split robes whipping about her legs, caught on the current of power.

'He's gone, Della,' Byrne said, lifting her voice a little to be heard over the snap of magic. 'Tellamoth—'

'Why are you here?' Della ignored her, attention on Shane on the other side of the cubicle. 'Why did you come?' Despite the magic ripping the air around her, Della's voice was soft, a sweet murmur that caressed the eardrums.

Shane swayed, his expression turning slack, eyes glazing as delicate twists of azure magic, Della's magic, wound through his ears.

'Della?' Alarm rose in Byrne's chest. 'What are you doing?'

Her best friend's dark-brown eyes didn't shift from Shane, and her voice still caressed the mind, but her words were for Byrne. 'What's it look like? I'm asking him questions.'

Lightning cracked around Della's hand where she gripped the staff, her tattoos glowing from within, and the magic holding Shane captive pulsed with it.

'That's a lot of magic for some questions,' Byrne said.

Della blinked, and for just a second, her eyes shifted from Shane to Byrne, before she studied her hands. 'Shit,' she said, voice losing some of its power-enhanced echo. 'Sorry.'

The lightning died and Della's tattoos lost some of their inner glow.

At her side, Shane shook his head and frowned as Della's magic loosened its hold on his mind. 'What the fuck is going—?'

Byrne interrupted him, turning him around and pinning his shoulder to the side of the cubicle. He was taller than her, she'd known that, but never really appreciated it, not until now, with just centimetres between them. She had to look up, just a couple of inches, but it seemed more, seemed like feet, and suddenly she was a little too aware of just being in her underwear, of the way her wet hair stuck to her cheek and chest.

The Sword raked fingers down her psyche, and Byrne shook her and the awareness away. Not the time. 'Why are you here, Shane?'

He frowned. 'I forgot my water bottle in the gym. Came back for it and saw a guy creeping about, so I followed him into the bathroom.' He reached up to dislodge her hand from his shoulder, and scowled when she didn't let him, pressing harder instead.

'You should let me go,' he said, warning in his tone.

'That's it?' Byrne said. 'You saw a guy?'

'And then I saved you from getting stabbed.' His fingers wrapped around the hand holding him to the wall. 'In case you forgot,' he added, even as the bands of flesh and bone tightened on Byrne's wrist, and his muscles tensed in readiness.

Magic played around Shane's jaw, the azure streaks highlighting his cheekbones before dancing around his brow and forcing his gaze to the side. To Della.

Azure shone under the High Priestess's skin, not a bright as before, but still enough to make her glimmer, even under the bathroom's harsh fluoro light.

'What did the guy look like?' Della asked.

'I didn't see him.'

'But you followed him.'

'He was wearing a hoodie and there was something... strange about him.'

'Strange how?'

Shane cast his eye up and down Della's form. 'Well, he wasn't cosplaying like you, but he kind of shimmered and he had a knife.' He turned back to Byrne, hand squeezing her wrist. 'You going to let me go now?'

There was an unspoken 'or' at the end that question, a hint of a threat in the way Shane pushed against her hand, and she knew, without him saying it, that he was done being pinned to the wall.

Out the corner of her eye, Byrne saw Della shake her head, a short sharp "no" and "I have more questions", but Byrne dropped her hand and stepped back.

He'd saved her life, or at the very least a trip to hospital, and there was something about him, beyond the boy-band looks and muscled abs, that told her to trust him. Maybe it was the callouses on his knuckles, or the respect in his gaze. Maybe it was the way he didn't treat her like glass or was one of the few boys who didn't think her a freak, even after she'd spent a fortnight solid kicking his pretty white arse.

Maybe.

Shane straightened. He didn't smile, but he gave her a nod and the scowl puckering his brow and turning his jaw to stone, loosened. 'So,' he said, gesturing to Della and the bloody scratch along Byrne's belly. 'What happened here? A knife fight seems a bit extreme for a cosplay argument—'

Della's staff *cracked* against the tiles, the tang of burnt ozone once again filling the air as the lightning around her hands sharpened with an audible *snap*.

Shane jerked, and before Byrne knew it, he was back against the cubicle wall, only this time she wasn't the one holding him there. This time it was Della, or rather her magic wrapping around Shane's head, sparking off his teeth and plunging into his ears.

'Della.' Alarm twisted through Byrne's voice. 'What are you doing? Let him go.'

'He knows more, even if he can't recall it consciously.' Della's voice was back to echoing, the tattoos swirling across her hands and up her arms glowing, just like the ones under her eyes and down her throat. 'Besides, he's seen us, seen *me*. I have to wipe his memory.'

'Della, no.'

'Yes. It's for the best, Byrne.'

'For who? For you and Nova?'

'For us.'

Chapter 16

For us.

Bullshit.

Bullshit, bullshit.

Bullshit!

She ran along the boardwalk, sneakers smashing into the weathered, grey-brown planks, relishing the burn in her thighs, the salty rasp in her throat. The late afternoon sun beat on her arms, trying to bake the hair to her head, her long pony-tail swaying with every stride, a metronome for her anger. The heat and the hard wind off the ocean stripped the sweat from her skin as soon as it formed, leaving nothing but salt and grit in their wake, reminding her of other lives – a Celtic warrior covered in mud; a dark-skinned slave up to her knees in sand; a scared little girl hiding in bulrushes – but mostly it reminded her of the nasty dirt and gore-encrusted aftermath of battle.

It reminded her of Az.

And it reminded Az of— Deep inside, the Sword rolled, sharp claws scoring the membrane between them.

Darkness, Az whispered. *Pain. Cold.* A pause and then, with a pained, bloody hiss, *Tellamoth.*

Tellamoth.

Byrne echoed Az's hiss.

She kept running.

Her t-shirt, with the meatball-head blonde superhero on the front, clung to her shoulder blades while the music pounded in her ears from the phone stashed in the pocket of knee-length running pants.

One hand held a half-empty water bottle while the other clenched around the fury rippling through her chest, like she could reach into her heart and yank it out. Gather it all in a ball and shove it in Nova's face.

No, not just shove it, *grind* it. Grab the other girl by her nape and smash the sticky, slimy, acidic mess down Nova's throat and up her nose. So deep and so hard she'd never get it out. Not in a million years.

And Della…

Byrne snarled, and a runner coming towards her on the boardwalk dodged, stumbling as they all but leapt off the path.

The angry ball in Byrne's chest twisted, spun in place and sent a plume of betrayal curling through her ribs.

Della had helped.

Fuck Della.

Her feet pounded harder on the boardwalk.

How could her best friend *do* that?

Fuck. How could *she* do that? Had she just let Della wipe Shane's—?

Different, Az said. *Safer* for him. *Remember…*

…the boy in the barn, the shock in his wide, sapphire eyes when the demon ripped his heart out. The way his knees had given way and he toppled sideways into the bloodied straw, that look still on his face, staring at her as he died.

Another life, another boy, the same shock, the same blossoming pain in his midnight blue gaze as blood bubbled over his lips, clutching her arm and telling her… telling her to… she didn't remember, but there were more. More boys, more deaths, more eyes staring into hers as they glassed over with death. Az shoved them at her, half-recalled fragments of dreams, weaving a terrible, horror-laden tapestry behind her eyeballs.

Remember...

A final memory, the eyes arctic, hair a ragged spill of white on a marble floor, demon blood soaking the ends. Not a boy, but a man, broken nails scoring the back of her hands, her fingers wrapped around his throat. Squeezing.

But it wasn't the white around his eyes, or the desperate way he gasped for oxygen that held her. Wasn't even the few disjointed words he managed to force out in the brief moment her hands relaxed – *'don't make what I did nothing'.* It was the inky black staining her skin, a dark, hungry monster eating the pale-gold flesh, cold, the air around it smoked white with frost.

Byrne ran, no longer sure if she was chasing the mad or outrunning the cold, only that the high scraggly cliffs at the other end of Ganlan Bay were getting closer and closer, the boardwalk coming to an end.

The weathered planks gave way to rutted, hard-packed dirt, as slippery as it was gritty underfoot. She kept running, uncaring when the rutted path, wide enough for two, faded to a thin line twisting through the grey-green salt bush, her feet familiar with the track, the way the dirt gave way to shale, and the low scrub snagged her knees, leaving scratches in the flesh.

She ran up and up and up the switchback trail, the last hundred metres a mad scramble, with hands as well as feet, climbing over moss-slick boulders and more scraggly, grey salt bush scoring arms and chest.

Her breath came hard in her throat, and in the last desperate lunge upwards – hands skidding, knee colliding with stone – she could imagine fingers wrapped around her own neck, frozen bones squeezing her airways, tighter and tighter and tighter still. And they were her own inky-black hands, and the face above them—

She clambered up the last rock, hands and knees scraping over the stone, sneakers squeaking, sweat a trickle down her spine, and stood. She closed her eyes and an instinctive half-turn brought her face to the afternoon sun. The same rays that baked her head now bathing her front, burning the memory of cold black fingers from her brain, the brilliant red behind her lids obliterating the face struggling to rise.

She stood, chin lifted to the sky, the hand not holding a water bottle half raised, palm out towards that light. Drinking it in, feeling it seep through skin and bone, down to the membrane between her and Az.

The other recoiled, and beneath her... Beneath Az, the cold and dark roiled, its sharp, pointed fingers melting in the heat, taking some of the rage with it.

But not all.

Not the boiling anger that belonged to her, to Byrne. And not the stabbing pain of betrayal, of knowing Della had taken her memories, and not just once.

How many times? How much of her, of Byrne, had her best friend ripped away?

And why? For what?

'For us.'

'Bullshit.' Byrne whispered the word, felt the wind snatch it away. 'Bullshit!' She yelled it. 'Fucking bullshit!'

She opened her eyes, glared out at the cove spread below.

Here, atop the rounded bluff – Ganlan Bay with its fancy, restaurant-lined boardwalk behind her and Pier Cove ahead, named for its hedgehog-like array of piers and boats – she was alone. Truly alone. No Az, no Nova, no Suun or Fion or Della. No Rio, no Dad. No teachers. Not even the cold-dark.

Just Byrne. A girl, breathing in the briny air, hair sticking to her cheek, music pounding in her ears, thigh muscles singing the song of hard use, a bur prickling her ankle where it had caught between sock and shoe. Ordinary. Normal.

Except she wasn't. Ordinary girls didn't have their memories wiped. Ordinary girls didn't know a hundred and eighty-nine ways to kill a person. Ordinary girls didn't go to shrinks or run their lungs raw because their best friend reached into their brain and ripped out what was theirs. Ordinary girls—

We were never ordinary. Az, still cowering under the membrane, in the dark.

'I don't care!'

You should.

'Why? What was so great about us, about *you*?' The air came hard in Byrne's lungs and her heart pounded like she was still running up the bluff. 'You *died*, Az. You died and everyone died with you.'

No, we live. Images boiled through the membrane: Nova and Suun, mousey Fion curled up in a chair beside Della.

'This isn't living!' Byrne bellowed back, dredging other memories from the depths of her mind – charging an archdemon, ichor spraying her face, its oily scent eating into her nose, coating her tongue in filth; taking a hit meant for Nova, a massive fist catching her under the ribs; the sharp crack of broken bones, then flying, the grassy edge of the cliff falling away. More ribs broken when she hit the bottom. Crawling through the dark, unable to tell seaweed from tentacles, salt spray from blood.

There were more memories, more pain, more horror carefully packed under her nightmares.

It is better than this. And now it was Az's turn, except what she showed Byrne… what she showed her…

One second Byrne was on her feet, the next her knees, unsure how she got there, or why her face was wet, only that the scream still ringing over the cove was hers and the adrenaline that made her hands shake came not from excitement but fear.

That kind of fear that robbed a body of sleep and whitened hair. The kind of fear that lived in the deep, dark, cold places, that kind that would break her. That *had* broken her.

Broken Az.

We won't go back.

'Where?'

You know.

'No.' Byrne shook her head, muscles shaky.

You do. You just have to remember.

Remember me. Remember you.

Remember Az.

And that rang true, a tiny spark in the depths of both their beings that leapt up and whispered, 'yes'.

'Is that why Nova made Della take our memories?'

Silence, a certain weight in the pit of Byrne's soul as Az contemplated the question. *Perhaps*, she finally said.

'You don't know?'

Mur took my memories when she took yours. Della shone in Az's thoughts, the High Priestess's azure tattoos lighting up her friend's dark face. *And even if she hadn't, would you listen if I told you what I knew?*

'I—'

No, Az answered for her. *You would not, because you are scared.*

'I am not.'

You are.

More memories assaulted Byrne, of the gym and solitary workouts in the dark. Of punching bags and shadow boxing, never sparring with another person, no one who could bleed. Until Shane.

And something inside squirmed at that thought, even as that tiny spark pulsed, just once, but brighter than before.

Az shied from the light. Byrne ignored it.

'You hurt people,' she said instead.

So do you.

The confusion on Sensei Joan's face when Byrne told the older woman she was leaving. The disappointment on her Dad's.

'That's different, I'm protecting them. From you.'

You are me.

'No, I'm not.'

Yes, you are. Az surged, charging the sunlight, the entire viscous force of her ripping through the membrane.

There was no time for Byrne to think, no time to brace or curse or fight back. There was just Az, staring out her eyes, filling out her skin, slotting into tiny holes in the fabric of her being, little tears she hadn't known were there until they went *click click click*. It was… was…

It had been a long time since Az smelled the sea, appreciated how the rich, briny scent hit the back of her throat and sat on her tongue. Longer since she'd enjoyed sunlight on her face or a soft, chill wind in her hair. Since there'd been peace in her bones.

The ground was hard, the goat track they'd followed more grit than rock, but she didn't rise. The discomfort was a small thing, too trivial to call it pain. She knew pain, true pain. It lived deep in her soul where it froze her bones and robbed the world of light.

For now, she just wanted to sit here, atop the bluff. Not moving or fighting or arguing. Just being. Showing the other, the girl, how it could be if they wished it, if they stopped being afraid.

There was power in the two of them, like this, in being neither girl nor Az but simply *them*.

'Except we're not.' The girl spoke, but it was *their* lips that moved, *their* voice that mixed with the breeze. 'There are holes…'

And the girl reached, down and down and down, through the still open membrane Az had burst through.

In the pit of their being, the cold-dark reached back.

The girl shied, retreating into the light.

'Scared,' Az said. 'You're scared.'

'So are you.'

'Maybe, but I will use it and become stronger. Will you?' She turned, dirt and grit digging into her backside as she twisted away from the ocean, to the look out over the giant spit of land behind.

They could see all of Port Wyden from the bluff.

Too big to be called a town, too small for a city, Port Wyden sat on the pointy end of the peninsula, sandwiched between rocky shorelines. The Falworth Channel sat at its back, the man-made waterway winding from Ganlan Bay to the lakes, the thoroughfare all but cutting the town off from the mainland.

Just a few bridges connected Port Wyden to the larger world. Just a few bridges, easily destroyed.

Hands clenched on thighs, short, rounded fingernails dug into her skin.

'Why?'

'For when the battle comes and the Horde pours through, we trap them here.'

No matter how wide, how tall, how sturdily built, a bridge was no match for Asenath Uthor.

'But the people...'

'Already dead.'

'Not yet.'

'They will be.'

'We have to protect them.' The girl flooded their mind's eye with faces: Sensei Joan, Ray, Dad, Shane, even Rio.

'No.' And it was Az's turn to share images, of palace hallways lined with blood, of smoke and dust and screams, and finally of Nova, the Empress crumpled on the floor in her white dress. 'We have to protect Nova.'

Another image, a hazy outline of... something, a sphere shrouded in shadow, held by... hands? Talons? She didn't know, the memory lost with the fragments of her soul, leaving just the ghost of itself behind. But it and Nova were inextricably linked, and if they lost one... Az shivered.

'I am strong enough to protect Nova. Are you?'

Chapter 17

The darkness woke Byrne.

It was cold, so cold it burned through her chest, taking all the warmth, freezing her lungs, stilling her heart. There was nothing but cold, twisting through her soul, rising from the depths of her being, of everything she was… and obliterating it. Even the Sword screamed, pain and rage warping her voice until it was the howl of a thousand demons, the roar of a storm, the knell of death itself come to claim the Universe.

When the dark was done, there was nothing left of Byrne, of Asenath, of the Sword. Nothing.

Everything. Gone.

In their place... In their place....

Byrne jerked upright, bedcovers puddling around her waist, sweat beading on brow and chest. Her heart hammered behind her ribs while gooseflesh raised her skin. And the cold... Byrne hugged herself, eyes caught in the dream, still seeing that column of darkness and the hand, broad and long-fingered, reaching out of it.

She lifted a hand, clenched it. The hand in the dream looked just like hers.

A shiver gripped her middle, and she huddled into the navy doona, pulling it up over her shoulders and wrapping it around her back.

Moonlight spilled through a gap in the curtains over her bedroom window. It spread its soft glow across the pale carpet, picking out the old coffee stain and the bare spot under her desk, where the back and forth of her chair had almost worn the fibres through. That moonlight climbed up the chair's old wooden legs and crept over the shawl draped across the ladder-back, the silver light washing out the wool's vibrant reds and rich blues, turning them silver and grey. It hit the wall then, slicing through the night to spotlight the collage of photos and knick knacks pinned there.

So many photos. Old and new and random. Bands, cartoons, ticket stubs, memories of good times, of friends and family.

A spark drew Byrne's gaze back to the sash window as a breeze wound through the thin opening at the bottom, stirring the heavy blue fabric. She shouldn't have been able to see it, but there was that spark, a twinkle in the air as if the breeze itself had caught a slice of moonlight and carried it across the room. Maybe her imagination or the aftershocks of the nightmare played tricks on her mind, but for a moment it appeared as if the spark hovered at the end of her bed, beckoning her. Before Byrne could shrug off the doona it was moving again, looping and twisting with the breeze, to land on the corkboard.

She slipped off the double bed and padded across the floor, the cold biting at legs left bare by her old and faded sleep shirt, the thin fabric with its large black polka dots ending at mid-thigh. But she didn't grab the doona off the bed, just wrapped her arms around her middle and stalked the spark.

It wavered, a microscopic flame sitting on a photo partially buried under a silly postcard from her dad's last trip to France, and a strip of photo-booth snaps she and Della had taken at the Halloween fair last year – Della a sleek, sexy witch pulling faces at the camera while Byrne, with devil's horns and smudged eyeliner, laughed at her side. Under all of that, the corner of something else peeked.

Carefully, her hands shaking as much from the shivers starting to wrack her middle as the aftereffects of the dream, Byrne reached for it. Her fingers passed through the spark, and for a second, as flesh met light, something shifted under the dark and cold in her middle. A glimmer of light, there and then gone, spreading comfort and warmth like a hand on her shoulder, a voice whispering "it's going to be all right".

And then she was tugging the photo from the board, the sharp *pop* of the pushpin vibrating through her hand, the soft *clunk* as it hit the desk, and the image was in her hand, the spark gone, the warmth and reassurance with it. Leaving just her, alone in her room with the moonlight pooling around her legs, enough of it streaming over her shoulder to make out the photo.

Five girls clustered together, heads pressed close as Suun took the group selfie. Fion, Suun and Della linked arms and made duck faces at the camera, while she and Nova were pressed cheek to cheek up the back. She touched the two of them.

She remembered this photo, remembered the day, remembered rolling around the park chucking leaves and grass at each other. It'd been taken before the solar flare, literally *minutes* before everything changed. Not all at once, but enough.

She traced her and Nova's faces, how close they were, in the photo as well as in life, and now—

Now Nova was stealing her memories. Didn't even have the guts to do it herself, but ordered Della instead, ordered Byrne's best friend to rummage through her mind and take out bits of her.

Against her chest, the crescent moon of Byrne's pendant flared, sharp rays of light piercing the darkness even as a slick, oily sensation tramped up her back.

Demons.

And close.

She dropped the photo.

How close?

Too close, the pendant and the slick, pinching stomp of claws and feet across her skin told her.

Cold and dreams forgotten, Byrne lunged for her nightstand and her phone.

Her skin crawled even as ripped the charger out and pressed her thumb to the screen and cursed at the error message.

Her pendant burned brighter.

Hurriedly, she tapped out the unlock code.

A screech against her window.

She jerked around, fumbling the phone, somehow managing to catch it before it hit the floor.

Nothing to see through the thin slice of open curtain, just the moonlight.

Adrenalin made her hands shake and churned her gut, turning her knees to rubber even as the Sword dug sharp, claw-like nails into her soul, a hairsbreadth away. With halting steps, she padded the half-dozen strides around the bed to the window, sticking to the shadows, half-afraid to breathe.

She shouldn't be doing this, she should be calling Nova, or Della and Suun, yelling down the line that the Horde was here, that somehow, someway, they'd pierced the magic that protected their real names, their real faces. But something, curiosity or fate, or the cold and dark of her dream, cramped her fingers around the phone, kept her thumb hovering above Nova's smiling face.

Heart pounding, breath shaky in her lungs, Byrne pressed her back to the bookcase beside the window and lifted the edge of the heavy, blue drapes.

Six large black eyes in a grotesque yet delicate face peered through the main gap between the two curtains. The creature pressed its face close to the window, its breath frosting the glass. It was humanoid in appearance: one head, two arms— No, not two, two other large, hairy appendages rose high over the demon's back, too long and with too many joints to be human. They were spider-like. Thick, heavy, black dreads sprang from the back of the creature's skull, while horn-like protrusions jutted from its jawbone.

Byrne forgot to breathe.

A Black Queen, a tracker demon. She'd never seen one so close, only on the edges of a fight or skittering through shadows. Fast, agile.

Tricky.

Deep inside, struggling against the dark and cold, the Sword screamed. *Run! Now, while you can.*

But Byrne was frozen, as frozen as her thumb that still hovered over Nova's number.

There was something about the Queen, how it tilted its head, how the four eyes embedded in its forehead rolled in their sockets and pinned her in place.

It grinned, its face splitting down the middle – nose to chin – jaw opening like two bony wings, displaying a forest of sharp, shiny teeth.

Her pendant burned.

Glass shattered.

In the last desperate second before the Queen burst into the room, shredding the curtains with its claws, the magic burst over Byrne's skin, sheathing her in armour, and her thumb found Nova's number.

But it was too late.

The Queen hissed and sprayed a sticky, toxic, yellow mist.

Byrne tried to back up, to shield her face, but the cold and magic held her tight and she stumbled, the Queen's mist like droplets of acid on her face, burning through her pores, claws seeking out her brain. Darkness took her sight, even as weariness took her muscles, turned her knees to jelly and drew her like a magnet to the floor.

The last thing she heard before consciousness fled was Nova's sleepy, "Hello?"

Chapter 18

She lay on her side. On hard, cracked ground. No longer in her room. No longer anywhere she knew. The sounds were wrong – hollow and echoing; and instead of the gentle hush of street traffic, there was the rolling growl of fast-moving water and the *click click click* of claws on stone.

Wherever she was, the cold and dark had followed her, wrapped themselves around her, muffling the Sword's steady *thump thump thump* against her soul and the warmth of the amulet against her chest. All that was left was the frost nipping at her fingers and the *drip drip drip* just behind her ear.

The steady drip of water had turned her neck to ice, and cold had long since numbed her nose but the sulphur and burnt-hair stench of demons clung to the inside of her nostrils, and their greasy presence still crawled over her skin. If only she could get up. She needed to get up. But why? Why, why?

It hurt to think, to move. The Black Queen's mist clung to her face and every twitch, every thought was a shard of pain driving through skin and bone. Even her tongue, coated with thick, astringent funk, hurt. Moving was too hard, too painful. She'd tried, slowly creeping her hand across the ground – too smooth for rock or asphalt, and curved, just a little – and the movement, small as it was, had driven stakes through her skull. She'd screamed then, or tried to, a small whimper taking the place of the ear shredding howl in her throat. Now, all she could do was lie there. Quiet. Waiting.

Waiting for what, she didn't know.

For rescue? Was Nova looking for her? Had she heard the scuffle, or had she just hung up, consigning Byrne's call to a late-night prank?

No, no. Nova wouldn't do that. All Byrne had to do was hold on, hold on and pray the others found her, before... Before what?

Before *he* found her. The knowledge rose from the depths of her being, down past where the Sword clawed and scraped against her insides, down deep in the pit.

Who, she wanted to ask, but it was a silly question because she knew.

Tellamoth.

Who else had the power to command the Arachnids? Who else would serve the Demon Lord?

She needed to get up, to break free from the lethargy holding her down, but the bonds were so tight, and she was so tired...

'Wake up.' The voice, male and familiar, whispered against her ear, his breath a spot of warmth amidst the dark. 'Az, wake up.'

She would if she could, but the tiny pinpricks of the Queen's acid held her tight, each sharp droplet a picket holding her eyelids closed, digging into her brain.

A hand on her forehead, warm and broad, the palm rough and large enough to swallow her face. It was his hand, the voice's hand, and it turned her face upward.

Water like shards of ice *drip drip dripped* onto her forehead.

She gasped, arms flailing, uncoordinated and jerky. She found a chest, a face, pushed, but her muscles were jelly, weak and floppy, and he might as well have been stone.

The hands continued to hold her face, but now one scrubbed, roughly spreading icy water over her cheeks and nose and chin. The sticky, toxic residue of the Queen's mist sloughed from her skin in what felt like thick sheets. First her brow then her eyes and lips.

She could see, could breathe, and the spikes driving through her brain, hindering thought and action, faded like they'd never been.

Inside, the Sword roared to life. Byrne welcomed her, embraced the hot, furious rush, the strength pouring into her bones. She was on her feet, a snarl ripping from her lips, Ahriman's solid haft in her hand, its dark, smoking tip pointed at her rescuer's throat.

They were in tunnel, a storm drain, she could tell that now. Walls and floor one continuous circle of cracked and crumbling concrete, wide enough to drive two cars through side by side. A thin trickle of water ran down the middle, the ground for a meter either side of it stained dark by past torrents, the edges a carpet of green where moss and grass erupted through the cracks. More dark trickles ran down the walls, and thin roots burst through the ceiling – ragged curtains funnelling water from above.

Of fresh air there was none, only the dank, stale breath of damp earth and the dark, skin-shrivelling stench of demons. While of light... No openings through which the moon or stars shone, no streetlights, nothing save the washed-out orange glow of chemical lights, the small pale sticks scattered about them in what looked like a three-metre radius.

Just enough light to see, to make out some details but not all. Like the figure at her feet, Ahriman's ink-dark tip still held to his throat.

When she'd lunged to her feet, he hadn't moved save to spread his hands to show they were empty. Even now, he remained kneeling on the hard ground. That could have been the weapon at his throat, but his hands were steady, not a tremble, not a twitch, and his eyes... Her hands tightened on Ahriman, the runes carved into the glaive's haft pressing into her flesh.

She couldn't see his eyes, not really. Shadows obscured his

face and form, maybe it was the soft orange glow of the night sticks scattered behind him, maybe that was just the lingering effects of the mist blurring her vision, turning the edges to starlight. Or maybe it was Tellamoth, maybe the warm hands and familiar voice were an illusion, a trick to get her to lower her guard.

Trick. The Sword growled in the back of her head, her hands wrapping around Byrne's, her muscles urging Byrne to strike and strike now. *Quickly*, she urged.

No, Byrne thought back.

'Who are you?' she demanded, her tongue thick, her voice scratchy and harsh.

He didn't answer.

She cleared her throat, the sound half growl, half cough. 'Who *are* you?' she said again.

'You know who I am.' The smooth, confident tenor rang bells of memory, but nothing rose to the surface. 'Az.'

Az. Az. Az. Asenath. Her real name, her *before* name.

Deep, deep down, under the Sword and the dark, the spark of that before person flickered.

'If I know you,' Byrne said. 'Step into the light; show your face.'

'No.'

'Why?' She pressed forward with Ahriman's blade, just enough to shave skin and force his chin up. 'What are you hiding?'

'Lots of things, but they don't matter right now.' Hands still at his side, open and empty, he rose, and Ahriman followed, the curved edge of its blade never leaving the delicate flesh under his chin.

He was tall, tall enough he topped Byrne by half a head, and the way he threw his shoulders back made him seem taller still. If only she could see his face, or his hair or... or something. Instead, the shadows clung to him like lovers, and in the soft orange-white glow from the chemical lights, she couldn't even make out the colour of his hair.

'He knows who you are, Az. Not just this form.' He gestured with one hand up and down the armour encasing Byrne, from the sharp nanite-reinforced tips of her boots, up the battle-tights and skirt, over the chest-plate and to the pauldrons cupping her shoulders. 'He knows your true form as well, the one you were born into in this life.'

'Tellamoth.' The name fell from Byrne's tongue.

'No.' His shoulders twitched as if he wanted to step forward, but Byrne pressed Ahriman tighter, and the shadows over his face shifted, like they were following the twist of his mouth. 'Stop being fucking obsessed with Tellamoth.' Bitterness coated his words.

'He's killed—'

'Has he?' He stepped forward, and Byrne had to back up lest Ahriman slice his jugular. 'Have you *seen* him kill someone? Has he shoved a knife in your ribs?'

'He tried.' The old sock smell and the humidity of the gym bathroom swam in her nose and clung to her skin. 'He failed.'

'Did he? Are you sure of what you saw, or what you thought you saw?' He moved like grease, fast and slick, spinning away from Ahriman's blade, shadows sliding over his face and twisting around his form, the curtain of dangling roots parting around him.

She cursed and tried to follow, but Ahriman was slow and heavy, the two-metre-long weapon designed to thrust and slash on the battlefield, not the curved concrete confines of a storm water drain, and Ahriman tangled in the roots hanging from the ceiling. She dropped the weapon, the glaive turning to smoke the moment it left her touch, brought her hands up and—

Had the wind knocked out of her, the boy/man slamming her into the damp concrete.

Byrne gasped, tried to expand stuck-together lungs, even as she shifted her weight and—

Another slam, and this time she saw stars and tasted blood, even as her ears rang and lights popped in her vision.

'There's more to an illusion than magic, Az. You taught me that.' His breath shivered across her cheek. 'You used to use it better than most. But there's no time for that now.'

A breath, just enough starlight cleared from her eyes to make out the shadow of his face, the sharp slash of cheek and brows. Arms pinned to her chest, she reared back her head and—

He was gone before she smashed her forehead into his nose, and she stumbled under the force of her own momentum. Away from the curved wall, feet splashing through the little river, toes catching in the cracked concrete. Ears still ringing, head full of the hollow echo that came with being smacked into a wall.

There, in the corner of her eye. The man, or boy, whatever he was, whoever he was, standing arms loose, hands open at his sides. She spun, Ahriman re-materalising, its sun-gold edge instantly turning black, and *thrust*.

He dissipated, smoke on the breeze. Ahriman passed through air, slicing through roots and sunk into concrete like butter, instead of flesh and bone.

'There's no *time, Az!*' He spoke from behind.

She snarled, the sound ripping the air as the Sword rose through her throat, the other melding with her muscle and sinew. And for the first time, Byrne welcomed her, welcomed the dark, angry rush, the rage swamping her heart, the certainty sinking into her soul.

'Asenath died, little man.' The voices were theirs, deeper than the girl's and lighter than the Sword's, a strange echoing meld of two beings. The words, though, the knowledge and memories belonged to the older part, to rage and bloodlust spilling through the thin membrane that kept the other down. 'She took the High Priestess's place on the Wheel and it threw her into the dark, where she was ripped to pieces, her soul scattered across the Universe to leave just the dregs behind.'

Ice burned along Ahriman's length, spreading over the haft from their hands until the very air smoked with the cold.

They jerked it out of the wall, and in the same move rammed it backwards.

A grunt of pain confirmed the spiked end had found their target's gut.

They smiled, shifted their grip and their feet so the glaive's blade was at their back, and they could watch as they jerked Ahriman out of the boy's stomach. 'I'm all that's left of Asenath Uthor, little man. All that honour, all that righteousness ground to stardust.'

He crumpled to the ground, hands clasped to his middle. For just a heartbeat, the shadows slipped from his face. She knew that face, and somewhere, deep down beyond the Sword and the dark, the remnants of Asenath Uthor stirred. It was gone as quickly as it came, the shadows once more coalescing over the boy's features, blurring even the memory of them.

'I know you,' he said. 'In this life, in your first and all the ones in between, I know you and you're in there, but there's no time to argue it now.'

Anger rose, and they spun Ahriman, lifting the blade high, angling it to come down at just the right angle to spray the boy's lifeblood across the tunnel walls.

'The Horde's coming through,' he said, the words freezing her muscles as surely as liquid nitrogen. 'There's a portal in the old drainage system, they've been building it for months, carving out a cave large enough for a vanguard.'

Somehow, through the shadows obscuring his face, their gazes met and held, and something, a connection like a live wire, jumped to life between them.

'Whoever you are, Az or the Sword or Byrne,' he said, still on the ground, blood pouring over his hands from the wound in his stomach. 'Now's the time, what you've spent all your lives fighting and dying for. If you miss this, if you waste time hating me, *killing* me, all your pain, all your plans and all you've sacrificed will be for nothing. *Nothing*, Az.' He spat the words, the same bitterness that had coated his use of Tellamoth's name spewing from his lips.

'*I* will be nothing,' he said, quietly.

In the pit of her soul, under the rage and the cold and dark, the first prick of starlight shone. It reached for the connection, the live wire strung between them and the boy.

'I can't be nothing,' he continued. 'I *won't* be nothing.'

Her arms trembled, and almost of its own accord Ahriman lowered, while an ancient memory struggled to rise. A gleaming room, pale grey marble threaded with gold, carpets so plush her bare feet sank deep into the pile. A man kneeling before a fire, the flickering yellow and gold flames coating his features in shadow, his hands holding hers, begging her.

'Who are you?' she said and wasn't sure if it was the memory or the boy in front of her.

It was the one in the real world that answered. 'No, who are *you*, Asenath Uthor?'

Chapter 19

'Byrne!'

The girl's name broke and bounced off the cracked concrete tunnel, splintering into a thousand echoes. *Byrne, Byrne, Byrne.* The sharp crack of boots, the howl of a demon, the smack and bang of magic followed after. The nose-searing stench of burning skin fought the musty smell of damp earth and mildew, while new lights swallowed the orange-white glow of the chem-sticks.

'Byrne!' Again, the girl's name – *her* name – splintering in her ears.

At her feet, the shadowed boy/man flopped against the drain's cold, curved wall, hands clasped to his belly, blood spilling over his fingers in a dark trickle.

The harsh *phitz-crack* of distant magic and a pain-filled demonic howl accompanied the next brilliant orange flash. Distantly, the part of her not caught in the boy/man's gaze, in the connection snapping and cracking between them, recognised the hallmarks of Suun's power, the skin-melting fire she could call to her hands.

'Byrne, where are you?' Della's voice, a desperate call sliding between the parts of herself, prying them apart – Sword and girl and the other, the spark deep in the pit.

The drainage tunnel rumbled under them, and a howl, like a

foul-smelling storm from deeper in. A new, brilliant red light washed out the pale orange of the chem-sticks, turned the yawning mouth of the storm drain into a backlit forest of thin hanging vines and cracked earth. A wave of heat came with it, pushing before it the stench of rotten eggs and meat left too long in the fridge.

Byrne gagged.

'The portal's finished.' At her feet, the boy/man almost snarled the words. 'The portal's *finished,* Az! You have to hurry. Do it now!'

But she didn't run, didn't pelt down the curved tunnel towards that awful, burnt hair and sulphur stench. Her boots were rooted to the storm drain, her eyes bound to the connection between her and the boy/man that hissed and spat between them.

In her soul, the Sword snarled, even as Byrne whispered, 'What do I do?'

'What you always do.' The boy/man closed his eyes and slumped all the way to the damp and cracked concrete. 'Just hurry. I won't be nothing, don't make me nothing, Az, not after all I've done.'

Heart in her throat, adrenalin made her veins boil and her hand clench on Ahriman's writhing midnight haft. 'What have you done?' she asked, and her voice was small, snatched away by the howl, and it didn't matter anyway.

'*Byrne!*'

'Byrne!'

Della and Suun's voices echoed through the tunnel behind, closer now, so close. She turned, caught the brilliant azure and white-gold of their magic playing on a turn in the drain. She should wait, she *could* wait, just a few seconds for her friends to catch up—

No, whispered the Sword. *We have to finish it.*

'I don't know how,' she whispered back. 'I don't know what; you haven't *told* me anything.'

Trust me, the other whispered, while cold, dark fingers wound through her insides. *Trust me*, the Sword said again.

And then Byrne was letting Ahriman drop, the glaive gone in a waft of smoke even before she bunched her muscles and ran, sprinting away from azure flashes of magic behind, away from Della and the others, and into the crimson forest ahead.

The first demons came out of nowhere. One second the storm drain was empty of everything but the dangling roots and the hard *crack* of Byrne's boots against concrete, and then it wasn't. The small, Scuttler demons came first, the eight-legged arachnids scuttling out of the dark in a black wave of dog-sized shells and claws.

Ahriman was in her hand before she thought it, an arc of black sunmetal sweeping through the tiny Horde. Those that weren't sliced in two – tiny sprays of ichor flying through the air, coating Ahriman's blade as much as the weed-cracked concrete – scattered like rice, the knee-high demons spreading up the walls. They clung to the curved sides and then up them, little pincer legs sending up showers of dust as they dug them into the concrete, the dark tide sweeping overhead.

Byrne shifted, bunching her shoulders to bring Ahriman up over her head and—

No. The Sword in her bones, overriding the play of tendon and muscle. *No time*, the other said.

With the Sword riding her muscles, Byrne's head turned towards the drain and the red glow.

There, the Sword whispered. *The real fight is there*.

No. Byrne strained against the Sword's hold, arms screaming even as the tiny demons swarmed over her head, their oversized claws reaching out, moisture dripping off the serrated edges. As if in slow motion, she watched a droplet form on the end of one pincher, watched it grow thick and heavy, the liquid steaming even as it left the demon's claw and fell towards her face. It splashed against her personal shield, the magic shimmering and smoking fractions of a millimetre over her nose, the acidic, burnt-ozone stench filling her nostrils.

A jerk, and her muscles were hers again, Ahriman slicing through concrete as easily as the Scuttlers' hard shells, filling the air with ichor. Her shield smoked and spat under the rain of demon blood, but she kept moving, Ahriman's long-curved blade a scythe, decapitating and slicing, reducing the black demonic tide to so many twitching legs and shattered shells. Sweep, stab and stab again, every thrust accompanied by a fresh burst of ichor and jerk as she wrestled control from the Sword.

No. There, the Sword shouted in her ear. The other dug claws into Byrne's bones, trying to wrest back control.

She had to do this, couldn't leave the Scuttlers here, at her back, ready to ambush Della and Suun as they came up behind. Except the Scuttler swarm didn't end. Instead of thinning, the black tide of rounded shells and clacking claws thickened, with more Scuttlers climbing over the corpses of their brethren—

Don't make me nothing. The boy/man's words echoed in her head. The vision of another room, another person on their knees at her feet briefly taking her sight, obliterating the tide of Scuttler shells and pincers. Along with it came the memory of guilt, the ancient feeling stirring in her belly, making her guts squirm and her heart ache.

The Sword rose with the memory, sweeping through the barrier. *Della and the others can look after themselves,* the Sword said. *The other...*

The boy/man's shadowed face, the bitterness in his voice and the blood seeping over his hands flashed through Byrne's mind.

Don't make me nothing.

A final sweep of Ahriman's blade and Byrne was running, leaping over the Scuttlers, bouncing off the knee-high tide, shells a shifting pathway underfoot.

Soon enough she left the Scuttlers behind, hearing only their *shritz shirtz skritz* on the concrete, the fading chitter of their pincers. The red glow from the portal stained the tunnel, stretching first over the ground before sending fingers up the walls. The stench came next, the rotting eggs and burnt hair smell rising from the fog, twisting through the tangle of roots dangling from the ceiling. It coated the back of her tongue with slime and filled her lungs like a wet blanket until her breath came in ragged gasps, her lungs stopped-up sponges.

She stumbled, vision going black around the edges, the meat going out of her bones. Her knees were on the ground before she realised that her legs had given out, the oozing fog crawling up around her elbows.

There were things in the fog. They slithered over the back of her hands, twisted around her wrists and reached thread-fine tentacles up her arms.

The fog reached into her brain, making her thoughts slow, dulling the urgency pounding on the back of her skull. And maybe those tendrils – now wound around her elbows, extending their delicate black web over her biceps and reaching for her neck – were in there too, winding through the grey matter.

She had to get to her feet, but her lungs were stuck together and every breath thickened the fog clouding her thoughts.

There was something important she was meant to be doing, a pair of shadowed eyes and a bitter voice stirring the nausea-inducing bile of guilt in her stomach, prodding her forward. She could think, if only she could get a clean breath of air, but the fog was up around her nose and when she tried to lift her arms, to push herself from her knees, the fine, hair-thin webs wrapped around her biceps held her down and then drew her closer, as if for a kiss.

The world was mist-shrouded red and Byrne was drifting away, pulled along with gentle tugs on arms and thoughts. Not even Ahriman's cold hard grip could keep her anchored.

Remember.

The voice whispered, winding through the red-lined fog, creeping in on the sulphur and hair stench, tracing the tendrils wrapped around brain and arms.

Remember, it said, and that whisper was cold, cold enough to freeze the fog and form crystals in the air. *Remember*, it said again. Its fingers slid up her nape, through the haze in her head, hard and strong, the ends rough with callouses, nails sharp, and somewhere in the cold, came the gleam of an eye. *Remember me.*

Byrne shivered. *Who are you?* she whispered back.

You know. The fingers dug into her brain, icy daggers spearing her skull.

Pain exploded behind Byrne's eyes, lightning going off under her skin, and for a moment it was as if her teeth were electric, the cold so bright, so deep that it invaded the very pulp and made them shine – brilliant, rectangular beacons glowing ice-white through her skin. In that pain, memories flowed.

A man at her feet, head bowed, features shadowed, his body backlit by the inferno raging behind. 'For you,' he said. 'I did it for you because you asked. All you ever had to do was ask.'

Another memory, of an ornate, blood-splattered hall thick with corpses, demon and human alike. A different man, in white-gold armour. 'We'll hold to the last,' he said.

'No, just until you see the signal.'

'What signal?'

'You'll know it.'

The memory faded and another took its place. An inky dark deeper than night in a place without the promise of sun, where there weren't even shadows. It was cold, colder even than the fingers spearing Byrne's brain, so cold her blood froze and the liquid in her eyes evaporated. So cold, death itself was frozen.

A presence lurked in that absolute black, a figure moving through the soul-searing cold, brushing fingers over her cheek. That touch burned, left welts on her skin, a new pain to differentiate from the old, to make the ragged tears in her being, the fragmented bits of herself scream anew.

'I have broken you, Asenath Uthor,' it said. 'You can't protect her now.'

I will. The scattered bits of herself whispered the words – no, the promise – and it echoed in the dark, bouncing off invisible walls, shattering against the presence. *I will.*

Did the presence growl or laugh? The deep, throaty rumble. 'You will try,' it said.

Claw— no, nails dug into Byrne's brain. The memory shattered, shards of ice flying through her skull, embedding themselves in eyes and ears and tongue, anchors for the obliterating cold to drag itself out of the pit.

Remember, it whispered. *And do.*

The cold surged, and the fog, the delicate tendrils holding Byrne captive mind and body, broke.

'I will,' Byrne promised. The fog froze on her breath.

She was on her feet, the dark and cold in her bones, lending strength and power to her legs, her arms.

Byrne ran.

A hulking mass of tentacles and horns burst out of the red-rimmed fog. It died. Acidic blood sprayed across her face, sizzling on her armour, its grotesque, oblong head food for the forest of black things in the shrouding fog.

Another demon came after that, and another and another as she pounded ever closer to the portal. The storm drain first straight, then branching, and always that red glow lighting the way, growing brighter and denser with the mist and rising stench.

The demons grew with it, larger and more numerous, Scuttlers giving way to more of the tentacled monstrosity, each of them dying on Ahriman's blade. The weapon itself sang in the air, and it was like the cold in her bones was reaching out through the glaive, pooling in the runes carved into its haft, smoking from its tip. And it wasn't just the cold anymore, wasn't just the dark or the Sword, it was the remembered promise – *I will, I will, I will* – beating in time with her heart.

The boy/man's bitter *I won't be nothing* mixed with the dark presence's *You can't protect her,* and pushed her forward. Pushed her right through the last tangled root vines, the final wave of Scuttlers and tentacle demons, and right into the Horde's beating heart.

Chapter 20

The portal stood in the middle of a storm-drain junction. Four massive, truck-sized tunnels, each a yawning black maw spilling into an equally massive chamber the size of a house.

Cracks ran though the concrete, spiderweb-thin fingers trailing over the ceiling, thickening to finger-width gaps down the rounded walls, then hand-width, then foot and thigh until there were great rivers of broken stone and exposed earth at the portal's foot. Of the portal itself...

Two great columns rose through the red-stained fog, slabs of man-made stone piled one atop the other – like vans stacked on their ends – reaching so high they didn't just touch the ceiling, they pierced it, hollowing out a great, bowl-shaped section of the storm drain's roof. Broken roots and pipes stuck out of the bowl, raining soil and water that quickly turned to steam.

A mirage shimmered between the portal's columns, a flickering rainbow barely holding back the harsh orange-red of an alien star, scorching even through the shrouding veil of fog.

The heat sucked the moisture from her eyeballs, made her skin tight, and parched her tongue, leaving nothing behind but a thin film of gunk and the sweet memory of water. Or maybe that was the stench, the scent of burning hair permanently embedded in her nose, the rotten-egg smell coating the back of her throat.

It didn't matter. What mattered was the hulking four-armed demon coming through the doorway. The barrier's rainbow shimmer clung to its massive shoulders, caught in the sharp spikes of the armoured plates over its neck and shoulders. The Horde world's red sun gleamed on the hard lines of the cannon in its arms, the generator strapped to its back. Behind the Mammoth came another, and another slow and lumbering, unlike the fast-moving Scuttlers at their feet.

So many, there were so many…

Byrne teetered under the crumbled arch of the storm drain, broken root-vines caught in her hair, Ahriman smoking in her hand.

Hundreds of the small demons spewed out of the portal, a tsunami swamping the chamber's broken concrete floor until the grey-brown was an eddying midnight sea. The Mammoths waded through the Scuttlers, every earth-shaking step landing with the wet *crunch* of broken carapaces.

As she stood there, the Scuttlers turned, the small dog-sized arachnids with their hand-long pincers flowing over the cracked ground, coming for her like her boots where made of honey. Or meat. Those pincers would crack her armour like it was glass, scoop out the insides and feast on her marrow.

Alarm screamed in Byrne's brain, a belated caution after the headlong rush through the drains.

Fuck. That thought was all hers, just like the panic building in her gut, hot and acidic, but the force tightening her hands on Ahriman, shifting her feet and bunching her muscles, eager to fight, that belonged to the Sword. To leap into the midst of that sea was suicide the sane-girl-known-as-Byrne part of her acknowledged.

But the other part, the older, bloodthirsty part, didn't care. Because there, in the midst of all that bone-crunching death, was the portal, sinking its roots into the earth, growing with every pulse of its heart.

The cold and dark raised its head out of the pit of her being. She needed to be on the other side of that veil.

To kill the portal, girl and Sword added.

Yes, the cold whispered. *And no*.

She gathered herself—

'Byrne!' The yell, not from behind but one of the other tunnels, echoed in the chamber, accompanied by a brilliant flash of azure light. 'Byrne!' Della yelled again.

The midnight sea shifted, pincers and cannons turning toward the flash of azure and the brilliant burst of sun-bright gold that came after.

For a moment, all was held in check, Byrne and demons paused on the precipice of violence until—

An unearthly scream shattered the air. Madness and fury combined in a blood-curdling wail as Fion exploded from the other tunnel. Her blonde mohawk pulled tight, braided ends whipping around her as her twin blades sent demon parts flying, blood spraying in giant arcs of black.

The Scuttler sea surged toward the new threat, two of the three Mammoths' giant cannons following.

Byrne leapt. Magic fuelled her bones, carrying her up and over. The Scuttlers passed underneath, the remaining Mammoth – bigger and slower than the Scuttlers – shifting its stance, the fist-sized end of its cannon starting to glow. Byrne had a moment to appreciate the beauty of it, the drama, and then she was in the midst of the swarm. Landing with the force of a meteor, Scuttlers and concrete crushed under her boots, gore mixing with dust in an inky black mud that sizzled on armour and shield.

In her periphery, she was aware of Fion and Suun and Nova, heard Della's relieved 'Byrne!' echo through the chamber, saw them in the mouth of another tunnel, magic and swords blazing, laying waste to the Horde. But it was the portal that truly held her attention, even as she spun Ahriman around her, thrusting and cutting with the curved blade as much as the spiked end.

Demons continued to pour through the portal, spiked armour and sharp claws dragging at the rainbow veil and beyond... The Sword snarled, anger as much as fear pulling Byrne's lips, grim determination in the flash of gritted teeth, and the cold... The dark, obliterating cold poured through Byrne's pores found a deeper spot of darkness beyond that shimmering veil and said, *There*.

Who are you, *Asenath Uthor?* The bitter voice whispered in response.

The question echoed in her head as she slashed and spun, demon blood spraying across her face, the thick black stuff smoking against the thin barrier of magic hovering over her skin. She dashed it aside, ducked under a shot from a Mammoth's cannon, the heat from the orange beam sizzling against her nape, adding another layer of burnt hair to the ichor and gore already clogging her nose.

There, in the red and the fog and the stink. *There* amidst the Scuttlers and Mammoths and other horrors – *there* was where she needed to be.

There. The cold and dark grabbed her bones. The answers were there.

Another blast of energy from the Mammoth, cutting through concrete and Scuttlers like a wrecking ball. Byrne leapt out of the way, coming down hard on smoking Scuttler corpses and earth. But even as she crouched, Ahriman held at the ready, a giant wave of the black, dog-sized arachnids gathered in the Mammoth-made gully, pincers chattering, one Scuttler-high, then two, then three, the demons climbing over each other to get to her. Behind them... behind them the head-sized end of the Mammoth's cannon glowed, while out the corner of her eye, she saw one of the other two stop firing on her friends and shift its attention to her.

Fuck.

A mad, blood-curdling yell, the twin flash of swords, and there was Fion at her back, and there were Scuttler parts – pincers and long hairy legs – flying all about.

Another blast of energy took the first Mammoth in the chest, the brilliant azure light beating it back.

Who was she? She was Byrne, she thought as she spun behind the demon, trusting Fion to keep the Scuttlers from her back. She was the Sword, the older, bloodier part of her added as Ahriman severed the tendons in the beast's ankles, its pain-filled howl music to her ears.

And she was the dark; the pitiless, vengeful void.

I will, Byrne whispered.

I will, the Sword answered.

You will, said the void, as frost gathered on her breath, her skin, the tips of her fingers, and the deep, absolute dark spread from the ground at her feet.

The portal, the shimmering, rainbow veil, pulled her. There, they needed to be *there*.

Byrne leapt, Ahriman a furious whirl of smoking black, the air freezing around ankles and knees, frost rimming her hands. Behind, Fion yelled, pain in the sound, but Byrne didn't look back, didn't stop. She was flying and the portal was there, the demon world's red haze seeping through the barrier, its harsh, glaring sun filling her heart, her sight, her mind. And still... Byrne retook control of her body and twisted, arms and shoulders screaming as she threw Ahriman. The glaive flew through the air, trailing ice in its wake. It hit the Mammoth with the force of a freight train. The great beast's chest armour shattered, and pinned it to the side of the chamber.

In the half-second it took Fion to meet Byrne's gaze, for something much like shock to pass through her eyes, Byrne was gone. There was just the obliterating cold, the portal and the darkness gathering in her hands.

A shimmer twisted through the portal's red haze; white hair and dark eyes glaring at her from a rainbow-fractured face. A sword materialising from nothing, the sharp gleaming point aimed at her chest, ready to impale her as she came down. No time to twist out of the way.

Cold at her heart, in her veins. The obliterating deep rose from her soul, pushed the Sword aside, and swept Byrne up in a torrent of icy nothingness. And then... and then...

She lost time somewhere.

She was on the ground, smashing through the Horde, Ahriman back in her hands, its haft and blade black, cold rising off it – off her – in waves. And there was the portal, a half-dozen steps away, the ground around it turned to frost, ice creeping up its supporting columns.

How had that happened?

There, the cold voice whispered in her ear, even as it turned her eyes to the darker speck of darkness beyond the portal's rainbow shimmer. The answers were *there*.

Byrne threw herself at the portal.

Distantly, she heard Della yell her name, felt the heat of Suun's fire magic scorch her cheek under the cold spreading up her arms, down through her feet, turning the concrete to ice.

She spun, sliced a Scuttler clean through, dug Ahriman's spiked end into a Mammoth's leg, smashed another Scuttler clear across the chamber, a black bowling ball cannoning into its fellows. The veil shimmered an arms-length away; the foul, red, Horde sun a furnace crisping her face, the world's stench-laden air already clinging to her skin and gumming up her throat.

Just a step. Just. A. Step—

Shattered rainbows caught in the corner of her eye. A fall of white hair, the gleaming arc of a knife, keening as it slipped through her shield. Then pain and a hot rush of blood across her back, the sharp curved point finding the chink under her shoulder blades, carving its way down her spine even as she twisted.

Agony radiated from the hot, wicked line, up her neck, down her arm. Her knees buckled even as Ahriman fell from nerveless fingers, the glaive vanishing before it hit the corpse-strewn concrete, and a rich, bold laugh crawled up her spine.

Tellamoth.

She was on one knee, looking up, the portal looming large in one eye, Tellamoth in the other. The Horde world's nauseating red fog rolled around her chest, the sulphur stench reaching for her chin, crawling down her throat and clogging her pores, but it was Tellamoth she saw.

His fractured rainbow face, then his knee as it smashed into hers. The crack of nose, a fresh wave of pain, another of blood sent her sprawling backwards. And now there was the portal, fuzzing against the top of her head, the thin, multi-coloured barrier sucking at her scalp. A boot in her ribs flipped her over, another lifted her to hands and knees even as it drove the air from her lungs. It didn't matter now, she was almost there, the darker speck of darkness a hard shove away.

And Tellamoth, Tellamoth just there, his dark, perfectly tied sneaker careening at her face.

Victory. Victory would be hers.

Her ribs screaming, lungs stuck together, oxygen a distant memory, she twisted, catching that foot as it cracked another rib. New pain engulfed her chest, a sharp spike piercing her insides, bringing a hot rush of blood to her lips.

Az looked up, caught Tellamoth's gaze through the illusion concealing his features, and smiled with bloodied teeth. Did she look now as she had then, in that broken, frozen memory? Had Tellamoth been able to see her in that utter darkness? Had he heard her promise? Did he remember?

'I've broken you,' he said. 'You can't save her now.'

'I can,' she'd whispered back.

She wheezed in a breath.

'I can,' she said aloud.

Tellamoth's eyes narrowed.

And she would.

Now.

She rolled, a hard, sharp *crunch* into his legs.

He fell. She kept rolling, up onto her hands and knees, nothing but starlight, dark jeans and Tellamoth in her eyes. His illusion pulled at her, pops and wheezes trying desperately to drag her attention away, but she knew what she wanted, knew where to go, and soon enough her forearm was crushing his larynx, and she was snarling into that masked face, watching his eyes roll back in his head.

His fingers clawed at her eyes, nails leaving ragged marks in her cheeks, but she didn't let go, just buried her face in his neck and held on. Just a minute, just enough time for him to pass out, oxygen to fill her lungs and her eyes to clear. Then just half a second to wrap him up in her arms and shove them both through the portal, and then to the darker darkness beyond—

'Byrne!' Nova, her bright sunburst-magic stealing Az's breath, loosening her hold just a bit as memories crashed through her mind. 'No!'

Hungry for the warmth, Az reached for them, but even as her mental fingers brushed scattered fragments, teased her with answers, hands gripped her shoulders, and yanked her back. Mentally and physically, ripping not just the memory but Tellamoth from her grasp.

There was no breath to snarl her rage and barely enough strength under the pain suffusing her chest to twist out of her captor's grip – out of Nova's grip, her sister-from-another-lifetime's eyes wide and desperate, but not focused on her, on Az. No, the desperation, the fear, that was all for...

She continued turning, Ahriman already condensing out of the smoke and cold in her hand, the glaive lifted over her head, the long, curved blade eating the light.

All the concern in Nova's face was for Tellamoth.

Fucking Tellamoth.

The bastard had found her. Wound his way into Nova's heart.

'You can't protect her.'
I will. I will.

Only to see azure light taking her prize, smashing into the ground where Tellamoth lay— Except he wasn't there, nothing but the illusion of him shredding under the might of Mur's magic.

And even as she drew in air to scream the thwarted fury in her soul, a different bolt of light hit the portal. A delicate white-gold that burned like the sun, searing flesh and rock even as it flooded the portal's shimmering rainbow barrier and *popped* it.

Between one heartbeat and the next, the portal vanished, taking the Horde home world and that darker speck of darkness with it.

Az was silent.

Cracks shot up the two pillars that had framed the portal, seeming to come from the earth itself, until the columns were a crazed mess of concrete and soil. The crazing didn't stop there. It spread across the roof – the broken pipes no longer raining just water but dirt as well – and down the walls, adding to the gaping holes already there. Cracks upon cracks upon cracks, adding to and growing themselves.

No.

A chunk of earth the size of a large dog crashed at her feet, damp soil and tiny stones splattering over her legs, a thick wet chunk smacking her in the mouth.

No, she thought again, louder and harder this time. 'No,' she said aloud, the word a frosty breath in the humid air. She'd been so close.

So.

Close.

Distantly, she felt more clods of dirt rain around her, the sticky *splot* of wet earth sticking to cheeks and armour. At the same time, she was aware of the remaining demons attacking; the Scuttlers' pointed feet *scricking* on chunks of concrete, their sharp, hand-sized pincers clacking madly, the Mammoths' ground-shuddering footsteps, the whine and crack of their cannons. Fion's war cry shivered in her ears, the brilliant burst of Suun's magic warmed her flesh, Nova's sun-bright halo dazzled her eyes and Della's hand on her arm, her desperate cry of 'Byrne! Byrne, snap out of it! We need you!' drove some so the cold from her bones. But nothing – *nothing* – could tear her from the collapsing portal and the beaconing darkness beyond.

Gone now.

Gone.

Just like Tellamoth. Ripped away in a shimmer of magic.

She remembered the rainbow obscuring Tellamoth's face.

Illusion, everything was an illusion.

Everything.

A shadow knocked Az out of the way as the roof come crumbling down. She hit the hard, corpse-strewn ground, a Scuttler carapace *crunching* under the impact, her head smacking concrete leaving the iron tang of blood on her throat. Stars obscured her vision as the cavern collapsed, dirt and rubble burying the portal, smothering the stench of sulphur and burnt hair, filling it instead with the damp scent of earth and dust, the cloying wetness of the sea-born midnight fog.

Chapter 21

Stars shone through the hole in the cavern roof and demons poured through it, up into the real world beyond, while Az stared at the earth and rubble that had buried her hopes.

Nova and Suun shot up into the starry sky, comets leaving fiery trails in their wake, while Fion leapt in great bounds, first atop the buried portal, then on a Mammoth's shoulders until she disappeared through the hole above.

And still Az only had eyes for the mound. The portal's shimmer still clung to broken bits of concrete, tattered rainbow streamers, while the red, furnace-like haze of the demon home-world dissipated into the chill, brine-laden air pouring through the gap in the roof.

'Byrne!' Mur's hand on her arm, yanking her around as an angry orange bolt turned concrete and earth into flying shards. And then moonlight, coalescing around her form and then…

And then the *between* place, where everything was nothing and nothing was everything. The deep, dark, obliterating cold pulling at her bones, creeping over her flesh, screaming in her ear—

And then a different kind of scream, the shrill screech of arachnids, the thundering whine and bellow of cannons, Fion's manic shriek.

A rich, green oval turned into a battlefield, the surrounding bleachers already smoking. Nova, a blazing sun at its centre, her sword in hand, a fiery extension of her being first here and then there, striking demons down even as she drew them to her, like a rolling shadow drawn by the light.

And there, Suun, the fire in her hands a brilliant silvery contrast to Nova's golden radiance, but still deadly. Earth and grass turned to ash with every blast of magic, arachnids to glassy shells. As Az watched, Suun sent a fireball into the sky, straight into the chest of an eel-headed Valous demon. The flyer screeched even as it died, its leathery, bat-like wings crumbling, hitting the ground in an explosion of dirt and wood as it took out a goal post.

Fion was at Suun's back, twin blades taking limbs and heads, and there, just there… A rainbow ripple.

Az was moving, ripping away from Della, Ahriman black and heartless in her hands. Stab, spin, slash, stab. Over and over and over again, her eyes on the ripple.

So close, she'd been so close at the portal.

Tellamoth was closer.

'You can't save her.'

She would this time.

Darkness on the back of her neck.

'You'll try.'

She whipped around, black and gold tabard twisting around her legs and frost flowing in her wake like tattered flags. And it wasn't Ahriman this time, but the void, flowing through her fingers and forming a blade even as she stabbed—

And met black, fuzzy flesh. Blood gushed over her knuckles, the Black Queen's hairy mandibles *clack clacking* against her vambraces, its oversized black eyes wide.

A cold breath on her neck. *'There's more to illusion than magic.'* A different voice?

It didn't matter.

Az tore the void-blade from the Queen's neck, barely noticing the demon's head flop from its shoulders, and twisted to face the new threat. Found another demon, an arachnid reared up on its hind legs, pincers snapping at her face.

The dark, cold blade demolished that one too.

'*Don't make me nothing.*'

Another twist, another stab, more ichor coating her hands, sizzling just above her armour-clad skin.

There, the rainbow in the corner of Az's eye, no longer circling Nova, but weaving through the Horde towards her. As soon as she turned, void-blade ice in her hand, it was gone.

Az snarled.

A laugh, like shredded skin on bitumen. 'You made him nothing a long time ago, Asenath Uthor.'

The air shimmered on her other side.

She spun and jabbed at air.

'Then I made *you* nothing.' The laugh and a cold slice of pain across her cheek followed by the hot rush of blood. 'Seems fair, doesn't it?'

Movement behind. Az already leaping, arms and legs corkscrewing, her tabard and long hair merging with the tattered, cold streamers flowing in her wake. The void-blade reformed from nothing as she twisted over her assailant, striking downwards with all the force of gravity and her own armour and magic fuelled strength—

Only to meet the Scuttler trio at her back, slamming through shells and bright green turf.

'Tellamoth!' She screamed. 'Show yourself!'

Another laugh, another slice across her face, the chill setting in and spreading through her cheekbone even as it spun her about. Nothing, no Tellamoth, no wave of pale hair, just the college oval, the massive sinkhole at her back, demons ripping up the once-green turf, Medea standing atop the far bleachers, the wooden seats ablaze everywhere except for the bubble of magic around her.

A pivot and there it was, the shimmer, a mirage barely seen in the dark predawn, with only the old stadium lights to see by.

Az roared even as she stabbed— and jerked to a halt, the void-blade's curved tip grinding sparks off the sparkling magic shield that sprang into existence between her and Tellamoth's shifting face.

'You had your chance at the portal, Asenath.' His voice didn't even strain, as if holding a shield against a void-blade was an easy thing, as if it couldn't tear even Della's magic apart. Lies. Illusion. 'You blew it,' he said.

She gritted her teeth and pushed the blade harder into the sparkling shield. 'I'll. End. You.' She forced the words out, summoning every ounce of strength in the girl's finely-honed body until the muscles stood out in her back and arms, until her thighs strained and her heart beat hard.

Sparkling shield and Tellamoth vanished, Az stumbling forward, almost smashing to her knees under the weight of her own momentum. Instead of landing face first in the torn, bloody earth, she tucked her head and rolled, attention already on the flicker of movement on her right.

Coming to her feet and this time not the void-blade but Ahriman in her hands, thrusting at that flicker, the night freezing in its wake.

A grunt of effort and a hasty shield, thinner and smaller than the first, met Ahriman's long curved blade.

She saw him clearer this time, could make out the dark slash of his brows and the sharp angle of his jaw through his kaleidoscopic illusion.

He smirked at her.

Az snarled and pressed harder, this time bringing not just her strength to bear, but the dark, obliterating cold as well. It came in a rush, exploding from inside.

The world froze. Ahriman pulsed in her hands, the runes

carved into its haft twisting, no longer just *black* but... But endless. She could fall into that black, it wanted her to fall in but first... but first she had to get rid of the light, of Tellamoth.

Another laugh – strain tearing at its edges – another stinging slash across her face, another rush of blood down her nose from the cut above her eyes.

'You're not strong enough,' Tellamoth said. The effort in his voice, the way his magic wavered and his shield thinned belied the words.

Both hands around Ahriman's haft, the dark and cold wrapping around arms and legs, bleeding not just from its runes but her heart, encasing every inch of her, whispering *more, more. More!*

Yes, she answered, and reached back along that torrent of dark, letting it fill her bones— No, letting it *become* her bones.

New strength filled her, endless and somehow... familiar.

She pressed harder against Tellamoth's shield.

A groan, his feet sliding in the torn earth. 'You're not strong enough,' he said again, but this time there was a hint of doubt in his voice, a question at the end of the statement.

She smiled back, a grimace with her lips pulled back from teeth and a vicious, bloodthirsty joy in her heart. 'I am,' she said. 'I *can*.'

And she pulled on that new strength, invited the cold in. It reached out from her bones, suffused her muscles, replaced her blood with ink, her skin with night, her breath with ice. She *was* the dark, she *was* the cold. All of her—

The darkness breathed. *Finally,* it said.

Tellamoth's shield *crrracked,* the illusions shrouding his face cracking with it. She knew that face.

He smiled at her. 'Finally,' he said.

—*almost* all of her.

A spark lit the shadows of Az's soul, a small flame flickering in the vastness, there and then gone. There again, burning bright, then gone once more, swallowed it seemed, until it popped up again, batting against the black.

No, the bright spark said.

It took control of Az's gaze, shifted it to Ahriman, the sun metal no longer tarnished gold but black, and her hands, fingers as black as Ahriman, like they'd been dipped in ink. Thick, roughly drawn lines rose out of the solid ink on her digits, reaching for the thin crescent moons wrapped around the black sun inscribed on the back of her hands.

Alarm caused the spark to flare, the tiny flame becoming a bonfire.

This is wrong, it said, and Az was surprised to recognise the girl's voice.

'Byrne.' She breathed the name, and watched the icicles frost Tellamoth's lashes.

He frowned at her, no longer straining to keep Ahriman from skewering his chest for the simple reason that she was no longer trying to kill him; the glaive's curved blade half-sunk into the churned-up earth at her feet, the area a half-metre around it – around her – frozen solid.

A snarl twisted Tellamoth's face, full lips curling over white teeth, dark brows over the long, straight line of his nose. He lunged at her.

A flash caught the knife as it came down, dancing across the straight blue-black edge and catching in the serrated teeth along its spine.

Instinct raised Az's arms, and she grunted as Tellamoth's blow slammed into her crossed wrists, her boots skidding in the frozen mud. The dark, sharp point hovered above her breastbone.

He was taller than her, just an inch, and he used that height to his advantage, both hands gripping the hilt as he bore down, all the while staring at her, hate and fury clashing in his dark eyes.

Az stared back, arms shaking, and tried to reach for the cold, for its strength. Mental fingers scraped its surface, the first chilling rush shooting through her muscles— And then the girl was there, yanking her back.

No, the girl whispered. *It's not right. He* wants *that, can't you tell?*

No. Yes…

…maybe.

But why? Why?

Around them the battle raged – Nova and Suun carving a dance of fiery death towards the demons holed up in the changing rooms, Fion and Della ripping apart those that remained on the field – but within the circle of frozen ground, only she and Tellamoth existed. Only the knife mattered.

'One more death, Asenath.' The words came out through gritted teeth. The blade shook and the tendons stood out on the back of his hands as he bore down on her shielding arms, and his eyes… His eyes sucked her in, just her and not the girl. 'You owe me this.'

I owe you nothing, she wanted to say, and yet she couldn't recall why, couldn't open her mouth to ask, because…

Tellamoth's gaze sank through her skull. 'You. Owe. Me,' he said again, the words smooth, soft, floating through her ears.

Her arms relaxed.

What are you doing?!

The knife pierced her armour, sinking through the nanites like butter, the frigid tip scoring her flesh.

'Stop!' The girl's voice, the girl's will strengthening her arms, catching Tellamoth's wrists and twisting. Both of them wheeling sideways, the dagger skittering into the battlefield.

The magic binding Az's arms, her tongue to her teeth shattered.

She yanked Ahriman out of the ground.

Tarnished gold washed through the glaive, chasing out the dark, and they were moving – Az and Sword and girl – a single unit spinning away from their attacker, bringing their weapon up and around and—

Gone.

Ahriman slashing empty space.

Tellamoth gone and the cold…

Az clutched at her chest. The soul-binding cold was gone with him. Her bones no longer tried to obliterate her flesh, the air no longer froze on her breath, and the power and strength… Vanished along with the girl and the bastard himself.

Fuck. She twisted about, frantically searching the oval for that tell-tale shimmer, finding nothing.

Where was he? Where—

Nova, the knowledge popped into her brain, he was going to kill Nova.

Az spun towards the stadium and the demon-choked tunnel leading to the locker rooms, just as a Mammoth stepped in her path, its cannon raised like a battering ram.

Chapter 22

Byrne ran. And ran and ran and ran. She ran until well past the rising sun, until she forgot what it felt like when her heart didn't pound or her muscles burned with acid. At first, she ran to outrun the screams, the look in Della's eyes, the betrayal that widened her gaze and pulled the blood from her face.

Or maybe that was just Ahriman, maybe the ghastly grey cast that overtook Della's dark-bronze cheeks was down to the blood seeping between her fingers.

At some point, Byrne ran not because of the look in Della's eyes, or the blood sticking to her fingers, but to get away from the cold and the dark.

From Tellamoth. From the knowing in his fractured gaze, the secrets twisted in his smile. From the stomach crawling shiver that came every time she remembered his fingers digging into the slices on her cheeks.

That's why she ran towards the sun, at first pounding down deserted roads, long hair and battleskirts flying behind her, armour-powered legs eating the bitumen in long, ground-cracking leaps, uncaring of the smattering of vehicles that hit brakes and horns. Ignoring lights and signs as she chased the first glimmer of morning.

A golden morning, not a heavy, red, sulphur-laden one.

Randall

As soon as the night lightened to dusk, the first cherry red rays of sun staining the sky, as soon as she'd caught the first glimmer of water, the first face-full of the salty breeze coming off the bay, she'd changed. Az and the Sword melting away, the ornate black chest armour and embroidered tabard shredding like smoke, sucked back into the pendant nestled just above her breastbone. The upside-down crescent glowing for a half-dozen bounding strides, and then, just like that, she was Byrne again, an ordinary schoolgirl pounding towards the boardwalk in the same nightie she'd been kidnapped in, her bare feet slapping against hard bitumen.

She hadn't stopped running then, not even when her breath came in ragged gasps or her feet ached. Not even when she left the road behind, or the boardwalk after that. Not even as she staggered up the thin, stony goat track that wound up and over Wyden's Bluff, rocks digging into her soles, low scraggly salt bush and a bare metre of loose shale all that stood between her and the crashing surf a hundred metres below. She ran until she didn't know where she was anymore, until she couldn't tell the pain in her feet from the one in her heart. She kept going until the agonised scream that had come out of Fion's mouth when Byrne jerked Ahriman out of Della's gut and her best friend hit the ground, was nothing more than a sick joke the seagulls played on her ears.

As much as she hated it, as much as that moment shredded her soul, that sound was better than the alternative, better than going back to that dark place. Better than returning to *his* hands.

Better than dying.

And so she ran, and when she stopped running, when her knees gave out and her lungs begged for air, when the brine of the sea covered the coppery tang of blood on the back of her tongue, Byrne didn't recognise herself. Didn't know the girl huddled in the lee of a salt bush, couldn't remember why she was there, staring out at the waves, the bright morning sun reflecting off the water. She only knew that her bones were cold, her fingertips blue, and that no matter how brilliant the sun's rays, no matter how long she basked under them, she would never be warm again.

☻

In the distance, he watched the girl huddle in on her herself. He watched her just like he'd watched her scramble up the fragile goat track, bound on one side by low grey salt bush and on the other by the sheer fall to the surf-strewn rocks below.

Seagulls flew overhead, winging for the boat moorings on the side of the bluff, drawn by the early morning fishermen cleaning their catch. Their cawing rose over the gentle crash of waves and he liked to imagine it was the girl crying.

The cold morning wind blew his long fringe into his eyes and chapped his lips, even found the gap between his sweatpants and hoodie, bringing goose flesh to his skin and cutting to the bone. Small, icy waves licked at his sneakers, adding to the chill making his sides shake, but he didn't move. Couldn't move.

He needed to stand here, the rising tide lapping at his ankles and eating away at the sand under his feet. Needed to stand here in the freezing cold to watch her.

The mighty Asenath Uthor, Bloody Sword of the Empire, scourge of the solar system, now a trembling wreck of a girl.

But not broken.

She should be broken.

Asenath was broken, he'd done it himself, caught her, reached into her soul and shredded it like so much overcooked meat. When he was done, only fragments of that once formidable woman had been left, easily manipulated, easily used and still…

He watched the girl. She'd resisted the command planted deep in one of Asenath's soul fragments, hadn't just fought the compulsion to re-join the Wheel and re-join the dark. She'd fought it and *won*.

Never, in all her other lives, had she *won*.

How? And why now? When he was so close to what he wanted, what he *needed*.

He remembered the spark in her eye and the macabre smile twisting her lips as they fought on the oval; that'd been Asenath, right down to the bloodied teeth. But there'd been something else there too, a vulnerability, a fear, deep down past all that hate... He'd seen it and hadn't cared. The acidic stench of demon blood had been deep in his nose and the hot, heady rush of impending victory had led artistry to his illusions.

Too much artistry, too much confidence, not enough ruthlessness. Not enough efficiency. Not enough *attention*.

It was the girl, it had to be the girl that pulled Asenath back. But the girl was Asena—

Feet splashing through the waves behind drew his attention from the girl huddled in the distant salt bush.

He didn't turn, but his gaze shifted to the shadow at his shoulder, as familiar to him as his own.

'You shouldn't be here,' he said.

'Neither should you.' The shadow shot the words back at him, and he knew, if the other had had the chance, a blade would have accompanied them.

'I'm going to finish it this time,' he said.

'And then?'

He straightened his shoulders, sought out the little cave in the cliff face. 'It'll be done; I'm pretty sure that's still what finished means.'

A snort without humour. 'I thought you were smarter than that.'

He turned at that – wet sand shifting under his feet, foaming waves swirling around his ankles – and met the eyes that had once been mirror copies of his own.

'I am,' he said. 'You're the one clinging to hope.'

The other frowned, dark brows shifting over a finely sculpted face. As beautiful as ever, in this life same as in the others.

'Hope's all I have. You saw to that.'

'No,' he said, and turned back to the bluff and the girl. 'That was all her.'

Epilogue

Ahriman glittered in the fading light, the golden haft of the weapon drinking the last of the sun's rays and seeming to glow from within.

Sitting on the rocky floor, Bryne stared at it, marvelled in the sheen of gold, the way it seemed to reach for her, brushing over her cheek in a warm, comforting caress and knew it for what it was. Sunmetal.

Az stirred in the back of her brain, trying to ride the memories to the surface of her thoughts, bringing the scent of roses and the warmth of— The memory stuttered, broke into a thousand pieces. Piercing blue eyes; long hair the colour of snow; hands, elegant and strong gliding over her back; arms corded with muscle wrapping around her waist; a deep familiar voice whispering in her ear, 'Remember me.'

She bolted to her feet, heart beating hard, breath coming fast.

Remember me.

Breath on her neck.

Byrne spun, Ahriman suddenly in her hand, darkness spreading outwards from her grip, turning the sunmetal black.

She scanned the cave, peering hard into the night. Nothing moved except the candle-cast shadows flickering with the breeze.

Remember me. Lips brushing her nape.

She whirled, Ahriman slashing the air, sunmetal black as sin. 'Who's there?'

The only answer was the cave, bouncing her words back to her, a million tiny fragments of her voice echoing in her ears.

Remember—

Ahriman sliced the night, the blade whistling as she turned to face the intruder, only to find her own shadow.

Remem—

'Stop it!' Panic rose in her chest, exploded in her voice.

The cave bounced it back again, and again, and again. Stop it. Stop. It. It. Sto-stop it.

'Stop it,' she said again, quieter this time, still searching the rock and shadows for... For what? For Tellamoth, or some phantom teasing her with a dream? Or was it something worse, was it the Sword bleeding through? Was that why Ahriman had stayed instead of turning to smoke the moment she let go? Was that why the sunmetal had been revealed, why it turned black at her touch? Was—

Remember.

'I'm trying,' she said. 'I'm *trying*!'

Liar.

Movement in the corner of her eye and Byrne spun again, Ahriman's deadly tip pointed at the deepest, darkest corner. Shadows rippled and split, her own form playing over the damp stone, seeming to grow larger with every flicker of the candle. There, in the fraction of a second before her shadow grew again, she saw it. A deeper slice in the stone.

Byrne knelt and fumbled on the ground for her phone, neither her eyes nor Ahriman leaving the shadow. A few brief swipes and with the steady white light of the phone's torch piercing the gloom, she stepped forward.

A different kind of adrenalin beat back the panic of before, made her heart sing, steadied the tremble in her hands and slowed her breathing. Her sneakers were silent, not even the gentle scuff of rubber soles on rock or the scutter of loose stones to warn of her presence.

The slice ran all the way up the wall; the torch outlined the edge of it in sharp relief and threw deeper shadows behind. She stepped around it, one slow sidestep after another, arm beginning to burn with effort of holding Ahriman steady with just one hand.

Slowly, the phone revealed an edge and then a corner, until she stared into the mouth of a tunnel hidden behind the outcropping of stone.

A breeze stirred the strands of hair that had escaped her braid, before reaching around to lift the hairs on her nape.

Nothing moved in the phone's paltry cone of light, not even shadows and still... And still.

Liar, the darkness whispered, reaching out of the tunnel to caress her face with familiar fingers. Suddenly, the word didn't feel like an accusation.

She stepped forward, feet still silent, hands still steady, although she shifted Ahriman, letting its point dip. The tunnel closed around her, only her phone's light preventing it from swallowing her whole.

The breeze came again, seeming to lift off the ground, a familiar hand skimming her hip, her shoulder, brushing aside escaped strands of hair. She shivered with fear and something else, a feeling that burned in her belly, that remembered mortal hands tracing the same path—

Byrne rubbed her cheek against her shoulder, scrubbing the sensation away.

Az. The same whisper, this time in her other ear, and the phantom brush of lips against her jaw.

She shivered.

Light broke the darkness ahead, not with the harsh blue-white of her phone but warm and buttery. She turned the torch off. The new light remained, the warmth of it reaching into her belly and urging her forwards, footstep after hurried footstep—

Byrne stopped, gritted her teeth against the sharp pull in her middle, and cursed as the soft *thwack* of her sneakers faded into echoes. There were so many things wrong here; the voice, the tunnel, the breeze playing with her hair.

Her.

She was wrong, broken, and half a step from losing control and letting the Sword free. She needed to go back, needed to find Della and Suun, to... To what? What could they do? What *would* they do but stick a knife between her ribs and plunge them into the Cycle?

Az. The name shivered through the air.

She started forward again.

The light passed around a bend in the tunnel, another outcropping of stone obscuring the source, a final chance for caution to scream in her ear, to stop her feet—

Az.

She took the last step.

Byrne didn't know what she had expected – a person, the voice whispering in her ear made flesh, smooth marble walls and a throne, a portal, a disembodied head, her own sorry soul trapped in amber – but it was more of the same damp rock and her backpack next to Rio's heavy candle.

Tension sang back through her bones and she gripped Ahriman tighter as she stepped into the light, careful to keep her back to the wall—

'Az.'

A sharp spike of fear, her body already moving, Ahriman clattering to the stone as she spun and reached for the voice, too close, so close she smelled the sweet mint of their breath. Hands finding shoulders, sliding around the neck even as she shifted, hip and shoulder ready to—

A shift, not hers. *Her* wrists held in fleshy shackles, a body pressing her to the cave wall, a forearm on her throat, threatening her windpipe.

'I didn't think you'd come.'

'I almost didn't,' she said and although the voice was hers, the words came from someplace else. As did what happened next.

Another took control of her body, wrapping her legs around her attacker's waist and arching her back, pushing his head to the side in the same move and breaking his hold. She was slamming her attacker into the cave wall in the next heartbeat, staring into a familiar face. Eyes the colour of glaciers challenged her from under dark, winged brows, the sharp planes of his cheekbones a contrast to the full, ripe lips. Hair the same boy-band white-blonde, except different, longer, half of it bound in tight cornrows.

"Shane" was what she meant to say but what came out was another name, escaping her lips on a slow, easy breath. 'Nilus.'

None of the shock rippling through her blood was in her voice, none of the confusion or fear that yelled at her to push him away and thrust Ahriman through his heart made it to her bones. Instead, she pressed closer, until she could imagine his heart thumping against her chest, until her lips brushed his.

She captured his wrists, spreading his arms out wide against the golden-veined marble at his back. And when had that happened, the small sane part of her wanted to know, when had the rough grey of the cave become luxurious? How had the stone and rubble become marble and silk hangings? Where had the elegantly flickering candles come from, the rugs, the window and the spindly fucking city beyond? Where the fuck was she?

But that other still had hold of her mouth, curling it into a smile. 'Hello,' she said, and delighted in the brush of flesh against flesh.

Shane smiled back. 'Hello.' He nibbled her lip. 'You're distracting me.'

'You started it.' She brought their hands together over his head, shutting his mouth with hers. And gods it was good, the press of lips, the hot thrust of their tongues sending shivers all the way down Byrne's spine. Her toes curled up on themselves and she pressed closer, no longer worrying about who else was in her body, using her voice so long as she had *more*, more of this, more of Shane or Nilus or whatever his damn name was.

'—Tellamoth.'

What?

She jerked back, the world fracturing for just a second, the light gone, the marble walls once again damp stone, and Shane/Nilus nowhere to be seen. And then it was back, and instead of ripping herself away from Shane, she was pulling back slowly, already mourning the loss of his warmth as she stepped away.

A cleared throat drew her attention from the heat in Nilus's gaze to the majordomo standing just beyond the shimmering veil of the privacy screen.

The tall, silver android with its slick black hair stood with its hands clasped lightly behind its back, still as the statues lining the great palace hallways just outside. Hallways that, with its pin-neat white, nano-enhanced suit it was designed to disappear into. Neither seen nor heard until needed.

And she *really* didn't need it now.

'Lord Tellamoth,' the domo said again, its face that smooth blankness only synthetics could manage. 'This is your requested interruption."

Her brow rose. 'You *requested* an interruption?'

He grinned, and the expression was rueful. 'I did, although now...' he reached for her.

'Should I return later?' Expressionless the majordomo might have been, but the sharp clear tones of its voice conveyed a wealth of disapproval.

Byrne stepped back, that other still controlling her muscles, but at least this time she was in agreement.

'No,' she replied for him. Another step back, but not before she reached out and flicked the long, tapered end of Nilus's nose. 'Work first, distractions later.'

The domo bowed, its perfectly proportioned, pearlescent face gleaming in the candlelight. 'As you wish, Your Grace,' it said, and just like that, disappeared.

Nilus slid forward the moment the domo faded into the background, one of the those deceptively graceful, quick movements that, like as not, caught her off guard. But not this time.

A hand in his face was enough to stop him.

Az stared him down. 'I said no.'

He sighed and spread his arms. 'Then when?'

She almost smiled at the resignation on his face. 'Later.'

Those hands dropped, slapping the black fabric of his pants. 'Damnit, Az.'

Now she did smile, turning away from the door towards the window-wall and the city beyond. 'You're the one who called the domo,' she said,

'I regret that now.'

She nodded, staring at the intricate dance of light and life that was the Imperial capital. 'So you should.' In the distance, hovers shot through the night, a billion tiny pinpricks of light twisting amongst spindly residential towers and the sturdier thrust of the business district.

'But since you did,' she continued, 'you should probably tell me about your brother.' She crossed her arms, the stiff black material of her uniform jacket practically crackling under her hands, the short cape dragging at her shoulders, just like the gold inlaid around her collar while the simple, tarnished gold circlet squeezed her temples.

Nilus was silent and when he spoke, it was right beside her ear, and the shock of it caused her heart to jerk in her chest.

'*The* Lord Tellamoth, scion of our house–' there was venom in the way Nilus spoke his older brother's title, hurts old and new in the arms he slipped around her waist '–does not agree with Her Imperial Majesty's latest military proposal. Surprise, surprise.

Even if the new tech works, he feels taking the fight to the Horde homeworld will cost too much.'

It would, but then it cost now too. Battlefields flashed behind her eyes, bodies strewn in mud, giant craters where the shells had fallen, scorch marks covering building and roads and towers in soot. And worse than the bodies strewn left and right, the carrion eaters feasting on soldiers and civilians with equal greed, where the outposts, the cities and the houses devoid of corpses, the ones where only blood and the rotten egg stench of a portal remained.

She didn't want to know what happened to the ones the Horde took back to their homeworld, hoped only that they were dead before they were dragged into that hell. But she would find out, would be the first to tread on that damned soil and wade through blood and ichor, if Jaya had her way.

'And is he convincing the others?' The politicians and aristocrats, the media, the people, every single mind he could reach and bring to bear on Jaya. It was the only way to dissuade the Empress from her plan.

Nilus's arms tightened around her waist. 'He's reaching out, doing what he does.'

Manipulating, twisting the truth until it screamed but never lying, telling people what they needed to hear to bring them to his side. One of the many gifts that ran in the Tellamoth line. Illusion masters, one and all.

Az nodded, still looking out over the twenty kilometres of mansions and botanical parks surrounding the palace, the night and lights turning them into a star-studded navy carpet. 'Is he succeeding?'

'It's difficult to tell. Most of the lords are keeping their cards close, and the media... You've done too good a job of keeping them safe; the citizens don't see the threat.'

But they would. Az's hands clenched on the arms around her middle, the now familiar cold, dread certainty rising from the depths of her soul. Soon. They'd know it soon, unless she stopped it, unless she did the unthinkable.

'And you?' she whispered. 'Has he convinced you yet?'

Warm lips against her collarbone. 'What if he has? Would you throw me away?'

'Depends.'

'On what?'

'How much you know.'

'I know a lot.'

'You *think* you know a lot.'

His lips smiled against her neck. 'And if I knew too much? What would you do then?'

Kill you, the cold-dark whispered from the pit of her soul.

No— She almost said that aloud, almost spoke to the whisper like it was a thing but caught herself. She wouldn't acknowledge it, *refused* to acknowledge it, even if – as she forced a smile and turned in Nilus's arms – the ice wasn't already creeping over the tips of her fingers, the dark seeping from under her nails to twist around her knuckles.

'We'll just have to wait and see, won't we?' she said, and kissed him.

Don't miss a book!

Scan the QR code or follow the link below to sign up for Belinda's mailing list and make sure you don't miss *Demons & Battleskirts Volume 2!* Plus, get a free short story.

I love keeping in touch with my readers, it's the second-best thing about being a writer (writing being the first best). Every fortnight (or thereabouts), I send out a newsletter with details about upcoming offers, new releases and extra special projects.

If you sign up for the mailing you'll receive exclusive behind-the-scenes extras, such as:

- free short stories
- deleted and alternate scenes
- previews of my upcoming books
- pancakes
- quizes
- and much, much more!

**Scan the QR code or visit the link below
to sign up and get your FREE short story!**
news.belindacrawford.com

Acknowledgements

Arck (she imagines writing in a really bad Scottish accent, with lots of spit), arck-knowledgments. I should like to arck-knowledge that: the Acknowledgments is the very last thing I write; that I am writing said Acknowledgments while rewatching season two of *Discovery of Witches* (hence the accent); and that Mathew doing the growly thing* is *waaaaay* funnier than the director intended.

I should also like to acknowledge the posse of fabulous people who made this book possible. As usual, I want to thank my awesome support crew (aka. family and friends) who put up with me bashing at my keyboard, totally ignoring things like dishes and vacuuming. I also want to thank my fabulous editor, Amanda J Spedding, also deserves a guernsey (and quite probably her weight in gold) for the fabulous work she puts in to making my books shine.

Also coming along on this journey were a number of very special people who believed enough in this book to support it via Kickstarter *before* it was published. These people are my Kickstarter Heroes, and I want to send a very special thanks to them all. They are: Anthea Sharp; Sarah; Sean Willson; Paola Khemchan; Katherine Shipman; CFH; Señor Neo; Dead Fishie; Emma Morris; Michael @mykesbytes Hricinak; Bobbi Schemerhorn, Author; Cole Killian; Tiffany Webb; Mike Dobey; Andre Jones; Richard Novak; Ryan Scott James, and K.R.S.

And last, but by no means least, I want to thank the fantabulous Iffet B., who has supported *Demons & Battleskirts* from it's very beginning as a serialised story on Patreon.

You're all my Heroes.

(*If you know, you know)

About the author

Physics makes Belinda's brain hurt, while quadratics cause her eyes to cross and any mention of probability equations will have her running for the door. Nonetheless, she loves watching documentaries about the natural world, biology, space, history and technology.

She's also a sucker for a fast horse, a faster computer and superhero movies. When she's not doing the horse, computer or superhero thing, Belinda writes sci-fi and fantasy for readers who like their fiction action-packed, with diverse characters, butt-kicking heroines and complex worlds.

As a certified crazy horse person, when she's not wrangling six-legged dynamos on the page, she's wrangling four-legged powder-kegs in the paddock. Belinda brings that same certified craziness to her writing with the kind of unexpected twists that'll keep you guessing.

You can keep in touch with Belinda, or just pick her brains about sci-fi via her website, Facebook or by sending her an email (she loves email).

www.belindacrawford.com
belinda@belindacrawford.com

Have news delivered straight to your inbox
via her mailing list. Sign up at:
belindacrawford.com/newsletter

DO YOU WANT MORE?
Take a journey through time and space
to go on an epic sci-fi saga.

THE HERO REBELLION 1

The battle for human evolution begins now.

Hero Regan is a freak; she hears voices, the kind only she can hear. Force medicated and isolated, her only solace is Fink, a six-hundred-kilogram, genetically engineered ruc-pard. They share lives, thoughts, triple-chocolate marshmallow ice-cream and the burning desire for freedom.

Their chance comes when Hero is allowed to attend an academy in Cumulus City, but in this super city nothing is as it seems. As Hero is drawn into an ancient conspiracy where two secret societies will stop at nothing to control human evolution, she must decide whether she's willing to risk the world for her freedom.

Scan the QR code or visit the link below to get your copy.
belindacrawford.com/hero

www.ingramcontent.com/pod-product-compliance
Lightning Source LLC
Chambersburg PA
CBHW020536120726
47904CB00003B/1106